PRAISE FOR INTERNATIONAL THRILLER AWARD WINNER AND *WALL STREET JOURNAL* BESTSELLING AUTHOR JOHN RECTOR

"It's no spoiler to say that this blend of horror and thriller sets its hook deeply and doesn't let readers escape."

—*Booklist*

"Rector does both bizarre and creepy quite well; though domestic suspense might be new for him, he is quite skilled at the thriller game."

—*Literary Hub*

"The true skill of *The Ridge* lies in the tone Rector sets from the beginning, one of constant tension and growing unease . . . *The Ridge* is definitely worth a read."

—*Washington Independent Review of Books*

"Reader[s] will not know what is real and who can be trusted, as they navigate the dark corners of Willow Ridge with Rector surprising them at every turn."

—*Out of the Gutter*

"Willow Ridge is a weird place, with weirder characters, and an even weirder agenda. Do yourself a favor and read all about it."

—*Night Owl Reviews*, Top Pick

"Rector has brought forth a new type of chill that once again proves small towns are not the peaceful little worlds they claim to be."

—*Suspense Magazine*

"An extraordinary, original, and deftly crafted novel, *The Ridge* is an inherently fascinating and unfailingly entertaining read from beginning to end."

—*Midwest Book Reviews*

"*The Ridge* is a creeping, pitch-black window into a suburban America like nothing you've ever read. The suspense builds with every sentence and you know something is deeply wrong with this neighborhood, and yet nothing will prepare you for the mind-melting final pages."

—Blake Crouch, international bestselling author of *Dark Matter* and the Wayward Pines Series

"*The Ridge* starts as a suburban noir and ends in *The Twilight Zone*. Each new revelation pulls you deeper, turns the pages faster. John Rector is one of the most consistently entertaining and unexpected writers I've had the pleasure to read."

—Eric Beetner, author of *Rumrunners* and *The Devil Doesn't Want Me*

"It's time to get on board, before Rector stops being 'the next big thing' and becomes the phenomenon he deserves to be."

—*Los Angeles Review of Books*

"John Rector is quickly becoming a master of suspense and drama."

—*New York Journal of Books*

"[O]ne of the very best new writers to enter the scene in a very long time . . . John Rector is a game changer."

—*Spinetingler Magazine*

"[Rector's] consistent excellence in storytelling is already proving his calling card."

—*Books and Writers*

"Rector brings some really impressive writing and strong characters into a genre that is often teeming with contrived, cringe-worthy dialogue and flat, unoriginal characters."

—*Baltimore Reads*

"Swift and savage and smart, Rector [writes] . . . superior pulp in the grand James M. Cain tradition."

—Max Allan Collins, author of *Road to Perdition*

BROKEN

ALSO BY JOHN RECTOR

The Ridge
Ruthless
Out of the Black
Lost Things: A Novella
Already Gone
The Grove
The Cold Kiss

BROKEN

JOHN RECTOR

This is a work of fiction. Names, characters, organizations, places, events, and incidents are either products of the author's imagination or are used fictitiously. Any resemblance to actual persons, living or dead, or actual events is purely coincidental.

Published by Thomas & Mercer, Seattle

www.apub.com

ISBN-13: 9781542091503
ISBN-10: 1542091500

Cover design by Christopher Lin

Printed in the United States of America

For Amy, always.

PART ONE

Magnolia James
141 Manitou Ave.
Manitou Springs, CO
December 24th

Dear Maggie,

It's Christmas Eve, and I can't sleep.

I've tried writing you a few times over the past couple months, but I can never find the right words, and all I end up doing is staring at the blank page and wishing I had the guts to call. I guess I'm scared you won't want to hear from me, and we'd only end up fighting. I can't do that anymore. So, I decided to write you instead.

But I don't know where to start.

Dad used to tell us that when we had

something to say, we should start at the beginning and keep going until we get to the end. Always keep things simple, right? So, that's what I'm going to try to do. I don't know if you're going to read this letter, or if you're going to throw it away or burn it. I hope you read it, and I hope you write me back, but I know that's asking a lot.

Starting at the beginning.

We're not on the road anymore. Mike and I stumbled on this odd little town called Beaumont Cove, and we instantly fell in love with it and decided to stay. It's amazing here, Mags. The town is right on the ocean, nestled in at the foot of these tall white cliffs that shine when the sunlight hits them just right. There's a road you can take to the top where you can park and look out over the sea, and it's one of the most beautiful views you can imagine. You would love it.

We haven't been here long, but the people I've met so far are the best. They're mostly old bikers and hippies, so you can imagine the vibe of the town. It's such a live and let live place. Everyone goes about their business at their own pace. I've been told the town changes in the summer when the tourists arrive, but right now it's peaceful and quiet, and that's exactly what we need. We live so close to the ocean that I can hear the waves when I open my windows.

I never want to leave.

Our apartment is in one of these extended stay motels at the end of a long boardwalk that runs along the sea. It's a nice place, and quiet. We got in for cheap since it's the off-season. The only other tenant is an old woman who has lived in this town her entire life. She doesn't walk very well, and she doesn't drive. I try to check on her now and then to see if she needs anything, but all she wants to do is talk. There's a local charity that helps her with food, and she has a nephew who is trying to get her set up in an assisted living home. She's very sweet and funny, but also a little lonely.

I started a new job last week, waiting tables, so nothing special. It's steady money, and I'll be putting some aside every week to send you. I want to pay you back. It might take a little while, but I promise I'll do it. Maybe then you'll forgive me.

There I go talking about things I didn't want to talk about.

I guess it's impossible to ignore the elephant in the room.

Maggie, I regret everything that happened between us. I know you were trying to help me and that I disappointed you, and I'm sorry. I said some things, and you said some things, and the next thing I knew I was gone and we weren't talking. I wish I could wave a magic wand and make everything better, but I can't. I know that as long as Mike is in my life you won't be, and that breaks my heart.

I wish you could see him the way I do.

Do you remember asking me how I'd feel if our roles were reversed, and what I'd do if it were you? At first I didn't want to see it, but what you said stayed with me, and I think it's part of the reason I'm not angry with you anymore. I know you don't think I had a reason to be angry, but I was. I understand that Mike and I haven't always been good for each other, and I hate that he has a temper, but I also hate that you turned your back on me because of him.

I'd like to think that if it was you, and you were with a man who I didn't think treated you the way you deserved, that I'd stand by you. That was our promise after all, don't you remember? I don't think I could walk away from that just because I didn't approve of your choices. Maybe that's the difference between you and me. You've always been stubborn, and I've always tried to forgive.

I didn't want to go down this path, and I didn't want to bring all this up, but I can't bring myself to erase it because it's how I feel. When you turned your back on me, I was crushed. I got married without you there, and I'm not sure I'll ever get over that. But a part of me also understands, because I understand you. I know you love me, Mags, just like I love you, but I'm not you and you're not me. My choices are mine to make, and yours belong to you.

Would I stand by and watch someone treat you the way Mike used to treat me?

Hell no, I wouldn't.

I'd want to kill him, and I'd do anything to help you get away from him, just like you did for me. But I'd also listen to you and try to understand. People deal with things differently, and Mike deals with his anger differently. He's not a bad person, and he's not a violent man by nature. He just doesn't know how to handle those emotions when they come up, but he's trying, and believe it or not, he's getting better. Now that we're away from Manitou, we don't fight anymore. Things are good between us again. If something upsets him, I can talk him down. We've learned ways of dealing with each other, and believe it or not, I'm happy.

I wish you could see it.

Okay, enough about all of that.

I'd ask how you're doing, but I'm sure I already know. You always seem to land on your feet. Sometimes I'll think about you and wonder what you're doing at that moment. I usually picture you in the office, running background checks, following couples to motels, always with your camera, always taking your pictures. It makes me happy to think that some things will never change, but at the same time I wish you were here with me.

I miss you.

I keep thinking that this is the first Christmas we won't spend together. In some ways, I feel like we failed Dad with all of this. And while I'm sure he would've been on your side when it came to Mike (he was always on your side with everything), I know he would've been sad about how things have turned out.

Okay, I'm just going to say this. Think of it as me taking the first step toward fixing things between us, or think of it as me being lonely and sad and missing my sister on Christmas Eve. Either is fine, because both are true.

I love you, and I'm sorry.

I'm including my address. I don't expect you to write me back, but I would love it if you did. I'd love it even more if you came to visit, but I know that's probably out of the question, although Mike would be thrilled to see us together again. I think he's getting tired of listening to me talk about you and cry.

I guess that's it.

I'm going to stop here and drop this letter in the mailbox tonight so I don't lose my nerve, and then I'm going to try and sleep. I hope you read this when it arrives, and that these late night thoughts of mine make some kind of sense. Most of all I hope you can forgive me the way I forgive you.

Life's too short.

Merry Christmas, Magnolia.

Lilly

Chapter One

Magnolia

The rain started falling an hour into the trip, slowly at first, but by the time we crested the hill overlooking Beaumont Cove, it'd become a downpour. The two-lane coastal highway, bordered by cliffs the color of bone on one side and the endlessly rolling sea on the other, was nearly deserted. I sat alone near the back of the bus, staring through the rain-streaked window, and thinking of things left unsaid.

A sign welcoming us to Beaumont Cove slipped by outside.

I leaned forward, unzipped the bag at my feet, and took out Lilly's letter. I'd read the words on the page so many times that they'd lost their meaning, so instead I focused on the scratched lines and curves of the ink. Lilly's handwriting was as familiar to me as my own, and as I traced the words with my finger, the realization of what had been lost settled inside of me like a weight, making it hard to pull free.

I wondered if this might be the moment when I finally cried, but then the man in the seat across the aisle spoke to me, breaking the spell.

"Beyond this place there be dragons."

The man smiled, his teeth the color of mango. He was older, gray, and had spent most of the trip flipping through a worn paperback, turning the pages with shaking hands and whispering under his breath as he read. Quiet, small, and unobtrusive. I'd almost forgotten he was there.

"Dragons?"

"The sign." He thumbed toward the back of the bus. "It should say, 'Welcome to the edge of the world.'"

"Beyond this place there be dragons." I nodded. "I get it."

His smile widened, revealing empty spaces.

I turned and looked out at the shadows of the town scattered across the hills and cliffs. From a distance, Beaumont Cove, with its low houses and winding tree-lined streets, seemed to unfurl along the coast, like a quaint Christmas village left to rot.

"Is it really that bad?" I asked. "This place?"

"Not bad," the man said. "Only forgotten."

I had a rule about not starting long conversations with people I meet on the bus, and as good-natured as the man seemed, I didn't feel like making an exception. I knew what was coming when we reached town, and I wasn't looking forward to it. The last thing I felt like doing was making small talk with a stranger.

Luckily, the man seemed to feel the same way, and he went back to his book and his whisperings without saying anything else.

I spent the last part of the trip watching the rain fall over the sea, and thinking about dragons and forgotten places at the edge of the world.

The sheriff saw me before I saw him.

I'd just stepped off the bus, and I was kneeling over my bag on the ground when I noticed him crossing the terminal toward me. As he got closer, his eyes grew wide, and when he stopped a few feet away from me, all he did was stare.

I stood and slung my bag over my shoulder, staring back.

"Am I under arrest?" I asked.

The sheriff seemed startled to hear me speak, and when he opened his mouth, he stumbled over his words. It took him a second to compose himself, then he shook his head and said, "I was told you were twins, but . . ." He paused. "It's really incredible."

I frowned, waiting.

"You're Magnolia James, right?"

"Maggie," I said. "Can I help you with something?"

The sheriff straightened, collected himself. "We spoke on the phone earlier. I'm Sheriff Parks."

"Okay."

"I wanted to come down and meet you in person, maybe give you a lift into town, help you get settled."

"Thanks," I said. "I can manage on my own."

"But . . ." The sheriff paused, frowned. "It's raining."

I glanced toward the windows running along the front of the terminal, nodded. "So it is."

"Miss James, this isn't the best part of town. It would be better if—" He hesitated. "I'd like to escort you to your hotel."

"I have the address," I said. "I'm sure I can find my own way."

"Actually, we moved you to the Cliff House," he said, practically beaming. "It's the best place in town, built right into the side of the cliffs. Your room looks out over the boardwalk, so you'll be able to see the ocean from your balcony."

"Why?"

"Because it's a nice view."

"I'm sure it is," I said. "But does the sheriff's office normally double as the welcoming committee in this town?"

The sheriff's smile faded. "We only want to help during a hard time."

"And that includes changing hotel reservations?"

"It's the same price. We worked it out so you can—"

"Maybe I liked the other place."

The sheriff's frown deepened. "Well, that's your call. If you'd rather stay at another hotel in town, it'll be easy to switch. There's no shortage of rooms right now."

"As long as I have a say," I said. "I'm still confused why you're involved at all. When we spoke on the phone, you never mentioned any of this."

"I received a call this morning from someone on your behalf," he said. "Do you know anyone at the police department in Manitou Springs?"

I was starting to understand. "A few people."

"Then there's your answer," he said. "The call came in this morning, asking us to lend you a hand. So, I'm here to make you feel welcome."

"I see."

"But if you don't want our help, I'll let you go about your business. Up to you."

I sighed and glanced around at the terminal. "I don't plan on staying long. I'm sure my original hotel will be fine."

"Then that's where I'll take you," he said. "From what I hear, they finally fixed their black mold problem, but I can't promise anything about the bedbugs."

The sheriff's face stayed cold and blank, but there was an unmistakable smile behind his words. I stared at him for what felt like a long time, and to his credit, he never blinked. Still, I let the silence drag on until it became uncomfortable before I broke.

"Well played, Sheriff."

Parks smiled. "The Cliff House is a fine hotel."

"I'm sure it is."

Sheriff Parks stepped to the side and motioned to the front of the terminal. "I'm right out front."

I adjusted my bag on my shoulder and started walking toward the doors.

Parks fell in beside me as we pushed through the large glass doors and stepped out into the rain. The cruiser was parked alongside the curb. He opened the passenger door and held it until I was inside, then he went around and slid in behind the wheel.

"You must know some important people in your hometown," he said. "We don't usually have cops calling from other states asking for favors."

"My dad was a cop," I said. "They're family."

He nodded. "I get it, and I'm damn sorry about what happened."

"Thanks," I said. "Me too."

Sheriff Parks started the engine and pulled away from the terminal. Once we were on the road, he said, "Ever been to the Cove before?"

"First time."

"Not a lot to see this time of year. Things are pretty quiet."

"I'm not here for the sights," I said. "I'm heading back as soon as we're finished. No offense."

"None taken."

We drove for a while without speaking, and I stared out the passenger window at the town, blurred by rain. We passed a sign that read **Historic District**, and Parks slowed as we moved along winding roads lined with restaurants, specialty stores, and gift shops. Every gift shop window seemed to showcase the same things: airbrushed posters, Beaumont Cove T-shirts, polished seashells, and wind chimes.

"It all looks so old," I said. "Do you get many tourists?"

"We do in the summer," he said. "But not like in the old days. Believe it or not, Beaumont Cove used to be one of the top tourist spots in this part of the state."

"What happened?"

"The world moved on," he said. "Once they built the interstate, fewer people drove the coastal highway, and we lost the traffic. We'll still get a few new tourists who find us by accident, but most people these days don't even know we're here. I like to think we're a well-kept secret."

I watched the town slump by outside the window, and I wondered how Lilly had found this place. How long had they been on the road, and why did they stop here?

Why Beaumont Cove?

Beyond this place there be dragons.

"I thought you could check into the hotel and get settled. I'll swing by in a couple hours to take you to the ME's office. Will that give you enough time?"

I was still thinking about Lilly, trying to imagine her life in this strange place. I knew what Mike had put her through back home, where she'd had friends and family to turn to, and that was bad enough. But the thought of her here, dying alone in this slowly decaying shadow of a town, broke my heart all over again.

"If you'd rather go tomorrow," Parks said, "I can pick you up in the morn—"

"Now," I said. "I can go to the hotel later."

Parks paused. "You don't want to check in first?"

"No," I said. "I want to get this over with."

Chapter Two

The medical examiner's office was in the basement of the Beaumont County Hospital. It was the tallest building I'd seen in town, five stories, made of brick, and painted solid white. Sheriff Parks pulled up out front, shut off the engine, and then turned to face me.

"I need to give you an idea of what to expect when we go inside," he said. "It's standard procedure whenever we have someone ID a body."

I nodded, letting him do his job, but I only half listened to what he was saying. Sitting in the parking lot and staring up at that white building, knowing Lilly was inside, made me numb, and when Parks finished going over what was about to happen, I barely noticed. It wasn't until he said my name and asked if I was okay that I snapped back.

"Are you sure you want to do this now?" he asked. "We can come back."

"I'm fine," I lied. "I want to get this behind me."

Parks started to say something else, but before he could, I opened the passenger door and stepped out into the rain. As I moved toward the building, the anger I'd been holding back burned inside of me, making it hard to think. I hated Mike for what he'd done, and I was furious at Lilly for staying with him after I'd handed her a way out. But most of all, I was mad at myself for not doing more when I had the chance.

I'd failed her, and now she was gone.

Behind me, I heard the sheriff's door close, and his footsteps move up fast. It wasn't until I sensed him next to me that I realized I'd stopped walking, and that I was standing in the middle of the parking lot, staring up at the hospital, with the rain soaking me to the skin. I felt his hand on my arm, gentle but insistent, leading me forward.

I looked up at him as we walked, but there were no words.

We rode the elevator down in silence, and the doors opened on an empty hallway lit by long fluorescent bulbs in the ceiling. There were several metal doors lining the hall, unnumbered, with two lights above each one, red and green.

Parks held the elevator door open, waiting for me to walk through. When I didn't move, he touched the back of my arm and said, "Miss James?"

I nodded, and we both stepped out.

He pointed me toward a set of metal doors at the far end of the hallway, and I felt a chill slide across my skin at the sight of them. I didn't want to get any closer, but when he started walking, I followed. My mind felt numb, and the only sounds I noticed were the buzzing of the lights above us and the slow click of our footsteps echoing off the dull linoleum floors.

When we reached the doors, Parks pushed them open and led me into a tiled room, dark and cold. There was a white autopsy table at one end, and four small metal doors built into the far wall. The only light came from an office in the corner. The door was open, and I could hear music coming from inside.

Parks turned to me, said, "Give me a minute." He crossed the room to the office, knocked on the open door, and stepped inside. I heard him say something, but I didn't catch the words. Then the music stopped and Parks walked out with a man in green scrubs carrying a clipboard. The man flipped through several pages on the clipboard, and he didn't look at me until Parks introduced us.

"Walter, this is Maggie James." He faced me. "Walter is Beaumont County's medical examiner."

Walter asked, "You're the deceased's sister?"

It was a question Lilly and I rarely heard in our lives, and it made me wonder what she must look like if he had to ask. The thought led to others until everything inside of me went cold. Part of me wished I'd taken the sheriff's advice and waited until tomorrow, but it was too late.

I told him I was Lilly's sister, and he glanced back at the clipboard before turning and flipping the light switch on the wall. Two lines of fluorescent lights flickered to life along the ceiling, and he led us around the edge of the room toward the four metal doors built into the wall. He set the clipboard on the autopsy table and read from the top.

"Lilly James, female, aged twenty-three years."

He nodded to himself, then reached for the handle on one of the doors and pulled.

The door slid open like a drawer, and I felt myself go tense when I saw the black bag inside. Walter walked around to the other side and waited, silent. Parks moved next to me, but I barely noticed him.

I couldn't look away from the black bag and the shape inside.

"Whenever you're ready," Parks said. "Take your time."

I nodded, told him I was ready.

Walter unzipped the bag and pulled it open.

When we were little, my father taught us both to swim. He took us to a public pool on a summer afternoon, and Lilly and I stood on the edge in matching pink-and-blue bathing suits with yellow plastic floaters high up on our arms, while he waited for us, waist-deep in the water below.

Lilly, of course, immediately jumped into his arms, laughing and splashing. But when it was my turn, I couldn't move. Every time I stepped close to the edge and looked down at the water, I'd start to cry, wanting desperately to turn and run. My father, to his credit, didn't try to force me. Instead, he smiled and said, "We'll try again when you're ready, honey." He knew that eventually I'd get tired of being left out, and that I'd want to join in the fun, but every time I got close, I froze.

It was Lilly who convinced me to jump.

She climbed out of the pool, her hair dripping in the sunlight, her eyes beaming with joy and life. She stood beside me on the edge.

"Don't be scared, Magnolia," she said. "You can hold my hand."

Then she reached down and took my hand, and all at once I knew that everything would be okay. I knew that as long as I held on to her, nothing bad could ever happen, and at that moment, I wasn't scared anymore.

"Is this the body of Lilly James?"

I could feel them watching me, and I tried to answer, but the words stuck in my throat, and I couldn't speak.

The woman lying in front of me was almost unrecognizable, and my chest felt so tight that I thought my ribs were going to cave in, crushing everything inside of me. I knew what'd happened to her. They'd told me how she died when they called, and I thought I knew what to expect, but I was wrong.

I had no idea.

"Miss James?" The sheriff's voice was soft. "We need a confirmation."

I swallowed hard and tried to keep my voice steady.

"Mike did this to her?" I asked.

Parks whispered, "He did."

I nodded, said, "Yes, that's my sister."

The words seemed to echo back to me, and all I could do was stand there as the medical examiner zipped the bag. I couldn't watch when he slid the drawer back into the wall, so I closed my eyes and waited.

When I heard the latch click, I felt something precious inside of me die.

Chapter Three

Thomas

She was alone the first time he saw her, standing at the end of the Starlight Pier and staring out at the black sea and the pink, swirling sky. She was young, with dark hair cut to just below her shoulders, and she wore a long navy-blue coat with a white fur collar that she held tight around her neck, protection against the cold October air.

She never saw him coming.

The season was over, and the shore was quiet. The last of the carnival rides had closed, and the day workers were busy boarding up the booths lining the boardwalk, securing them for the winter. Beneath the pier, a scatter of solitary beachcombers walked along the waterline, gray figures against gray sand.

He approached her slowly, stopping several feet from where she stood, and leaned against the wooden railing. Her back was to him, and he watched her from the corner of his eye, keeping his distance.

Patient.

The wind coming off the water chilled his skin, and he wondered how long she'd been standing out here. He thought about asking if she was okay, if she needed help, but every time he tried to speak to her, he lost his nerve.

Instead, he took a pack of cigarettes from his pocket, tapped one out, and lit it.

The girl stiffened at the sound and looked back at him.

For a moment they just stood there, studying each other. He could tell she was sizing him up, trying to decide if he was a threat, so he gave her his softest smile and focused his attention on his cigarette and the shore.

Eventually, he felt her relax, and she turned back toward the sea.

"Do you think people get what they deserve?"

Her voice was smooth and full, and it caressed something deep inside of him. He was so taken by the sound that he'd missed the question.

"I'm sorry?"

"In life," she said. "Do you believe people get what they deserve?"

"Do you mean like karma?"

The girl didn't look at him, but he saw the edges of her lips curl into a thin smile. "Yeah," she said. "Like karma."

He thought about his answer, but he didn't know what she wanted to hear. He didn't want to say the wrong thing, so he didn't say anything at all, and the silence grew.

Eventually she lost interest and began digging through her pockets.

"Damn it." She made a frustrated sound, then glanced over at him and motioned toward the cigarette in his hand. "Do you have another?"

He opened the pack and tapped out his last cigarette, handing it to her. She put it to her lips, and he stepped in with a lighter, cupping his hands against the wind. As she leaned into the flame, his fingers brushed against her cheek. Her skin was warm and soft against his, and he felt a low moan shiver in the back of his throat.

He swallowed hard to keep it there.

"Thanks," she said.

He nodded, silent.

"I'm Lilly."

"Thomas."

"It's nice to meet you, Thomas." She smiled, but he could tell it didn't come naturally. "You look familiar. Have we met?"

"I don't think so," he said. "I just moved here."

"On purpose?"

He thought she might be making a joke, and that he should laugh, but it was hard to tell. So instead, he nodded and said, "I spent a few summers here as a kid. I knew what I was getting into."

"A summer child." Lilly looked past him toward the boardwalk, her eyes faraway, lost. "It's a different place in the winter."

She was right.

In the summer, the boardwalk stood packed with tourists. The arcade opened every morning with a whirl of lights and bells, and the rides lining the shore spun well into the night. The breeze coming off the sea was always warm in the summer, and the air was thick with the sticky-sweet smell of cotton candy and funnel cakes. And above it all, the sun burned bright, and the sky shone a perfect, lonely blue.

In the summer, things were different.

"Do you live around here?"

Thomas motioned toward the boardwalk and Main Street and the golden lights of town scattered like fallen stars across the hills. "The Orion Motor Lodge."

Lilly's eyes narrowed. "That's where I've seen you." She pointed at him with her cigarette. "You took Ms. Calloway's place."

"Moved in last week."

"I'm there, too," she said. "Number nine."

Thomas touched his chest. "I'm in number—"

"Number three, yeah, I know, right across the parking lot."

"That's me."

Lilly studied him for a moment longer, then put her cigarette to her lips and inhaled deep. "What do you think of the Orion?"

"It's different than I remember."

"How so?"

"Just different," he said. "My family stayed there whenever we were in town. I think it used to be nicer."

"Like everything else these days." She folded her arms over her chest and ashed her cigarette into the wind. "Your folks must've liked the place if they kept coming back."

"Enough to buy it when they had the chance."

Lilly paused. "Your family owns the Orion?"

"They planned on developing it," he said. "They wanted to turn it into something more upscale than a motor lodge, but that never happened."

"Why not?"

"Didn't work out, that's all."

Lilly stared at him, and a dark line formed between her eyebrows. "If your family owns the Orion, does that make you my landlord?"

Thomas smiled. "The rental company handles all that," he said. "I just try to help out where I can, day-to-day maintenance, clogged pipes, blown fuses, that kind of thing."

"So, you're the handyman."

"As long as it's something small. The big jobs get called in."

Lilly didn't say anything else, but she didn't look away.

"I don't get paid," Thomas said, clarifying. "But I also don't have to pay rent."

"That must be nice."

Thomas shrugged and put his hands on the railing, staring out over the water. The pink clouds had started to break along the horizon, and the bruised sky behind them bled through, deep and dark.

Lilly followed his gaze, and for a while the silence filled the space between them. Then she said, "Where were you before you came to the Cove?"

"Just around."

Lilly didn't press, but she turned to face him, her head tilted slightly to the side. Thomas looked at her, letting his eyes follow the delicate curve of her neck. He imagined what it would feel like in his hands, how her skin would taste on his lips, how her body might move beneath his.

He forced himself to look away.

"Now I'm intrigued," Lilly said, leaning against the railing. "You're a bit of a mystery, Thomas from just around."

"Not really," he said. "I'm as dull as they come."

Lilly laughed, and this time when she smiled at him, it shone on her face, beautiful and pure. Thomas's breath caught in his throat, and at that moment all he wanted was to make that smile last forever. But then she looked past him toward the boardwalk and everything changed.

"Shit." Lilly pushed away from the railing and pulled her coat tight. "I've got to go. I'm sorry."

Thomas turned toward the boardwalk, following her gaze.

There was a man in a brown coat standing at the end of the pier, watching them.

"Who is that?"

"My husband." Lilly dropped the cigarette and crushed it under her foot. "It's getting late anyway. I should get back."

She slipped past him, moving quickly down the pier.

Thomas watched as she walked away, not wanting to miss a single step. She was almost to the boardwalk before he found his voice and shouted after her, "It was nice meeting you."

He thought she'd ignore him, like they always did, but instead she spun around to face him, walking backward, and said, "Thank you for the cigarette, Thomas. Maybe I'll see you . . . just around."

Thomas lifted a hand to wave as she turned and ran the rest of the way.

When she reached the boardwalk, her husband said something to her, but the words were lost behind the angry roar of the sea. Thomas saw Lilly try to slide past him, but then her husband reached down and grabbed her arm. He jerked her back before pulling her away from the pier.

Thomas watched them go.

He was about to turn away when it happened.

As Lilly and her husband crossed the boardwalk and started up the path leading toward Main Street, he saw her turn and look back at him over her shoulder. It happened so quickly, and she was so far away, that Thomas couldn't be completely sure if it was real or if he'd imagined it.

Except, he wanted it to be real.

Later that night, Thomas stood at his window and stared out at Lilly's apartment across the parking lot. He wanted desperately to see her again, even a glimpse of her, but her door stayed closed, and the curtains stayed drawn.

He spent that night lying awake in bed, staring up at the ceiling and picturing the way her eyes shone when she smiled at him. He could still hear the smoothness of her voice in his mind, feel the way it'd moved through him so easily, so intimately. The memory of her was so vivid that it was almost as if she were there with him, every detail of her seared into his brain.

The way her dark hair played gently on the wind.

The warmth of her skin against his fingertips when he'd touched her cheek.

The way her hips sang to him as she moved down the pier, begging him to follow.

But his thoughts kept returning to the last time he saw her, and how she had turned back to him, glancing over her shoulder, searching for him as she walked away.

Had he imagined it?

More than anything he wanted to believe it was true, that she had looked back for him, and that what they'd shared that evening at the lonely end of the Starlight Pier had been beautiful and real.

So in the end, that's exactly what he did.

Chapter Four

The next day it started to rain.

The storm rolled in off the sea, bending trees, flooding streets, and keeping most people indoors. Thomas spent the time sitting by the window, listening to the classical station on the radio and watching Lilly's apartment.

Waiting.

On the second day, the rain fell harder. Thomas considered going around to the other apartments to check for damage from the storm, but there was no hurry. It was the off-season, and there were no new tenants coming. If anything went wrong, he'd handle it once the storm had passed.

Besides, he didn't like the rain.

On the third day, the rain stopped and the sun came out, bright and warm against a clear blue sky. Thomas dressed and went down to the manager's office. When he went inside, the curtains were closed, and the room was cold and dimly lit. He kept the lights off as he crossed the office toward the desk against the far wall and opened the drawer containing the master keys. He found the ring, then left the office and walked around back to the maintenance shed.

The padlock on the shed was old and rusted, and it took a couple of tries to get the key to turn. Once it did, he removed the lock and pulled the doors open.

The air inside the shed smelled like dirt and wood rot.

There was a workbench in the back, covered with dust and rusting tools. Next to the bench, a dim line of rakes, brooms, and shovels hung along the wall. Thomas brushed away a mist of spiderwebs, then loaded one of the rakes, along with a pair of thick gardening gloves and a stack of recyclable paper bags, into a green wheelbarrow and wheeled it out of the shed.

He set the wheelbarrow in a small patch of grass next to the main walkway and stepped back, gazing up at the cloudless early-autumn sky. The sun felt nice on his skin, and he closed his eyes, letting the subtle warmth of the morning sink into him.

Then he got to work, cleaning out the dead leaves and branches left behind by the storm. He made good progress, losing himself in the monotony of the task. He almost didn't notice when the door to unit nine opened and Lilly's husband walked out.

The man wore dirty jeans and heavy work boots. He had a brown leather tool belt slung over one shoulder and a coffee cup in his hand. He paused at the top of the stairs to light a cigarette before starting down toward a blue El Camino double-parked in the lot.

Thomas kept working, pretending not to notice him.

When the man reached the car, he dropped the tool belt in the back end, unlocked the driver's side door, and slid inside. Thomas stopped raking and watched the El Camino pull out of the parking lot and turn right onto Main Street, heading toward town. Once the car was out of sight, Thomas looked up at Lilly's apartment.

He didn't see her, but he knew she was inside, and she was alone.

A voice, small but insistent, pushed him to go to her.

He considered crossing the parking lot and climbing the stairs to her apartment, but when he thought about seeing her again, his chest ached and he couldn't breathe, and he knew he wouldn't be able to do it.

If he wanted to see her, he'd need a reason.

Thomas ran through every excuse he could think of, but they all seemed so transparent, so obvious. After a while, he glanced down at the small pile of dead leaves and branches at his feet and went back to work, letting his mind reset. He knew there had to be a reason to see her, and if he thought about it long enough, the answer would come.

He was so lost in thought that he didn't notice Lilly had left her apartment until she was down the stairs and halfway across the parking lot. She wore a black T-shirt, and she was carrying a pink laundry basket filled with clothes.

Thomas dropped the rake and moved around to the side of the main office, out of sight. He took a deep breath, waiting for his heart to slow, then he inched his way around the corner in time to see Lilly pull the laundry room door open and disappear inside.

Thomas smiled.

He pulled the gloves off, tossed them into the wheelbarrow, and ran back to his apartment. Once inside, he went to his closet and grabbed the worn cardboard box he used for laundry. It was empty, and he felt a wave of panic sweep over him.

He was going to miss her.

The perfect excuse, lost if he didn't hurry.

He set the empty box on his bed, then went to his dresser and took several clean shirts and pants out of the drawers. He stuffed everything into the box, then hurried out of his apartment. When he got to the laundry room, he stopped outside, forcing himself to calm down. Then he pulled the door open and walked in.

Lilly was standing at one of the washing machines, sliding quarters into the coin slots. Her laundry basket was on the ground by her feet, empty.

When she saw him, her eyes widened. "Hey, you."

Thomas cleared his throat. "Hi."

"Laundry day for you, too?"

He nodded and glanced down at the box in his arms. The clothes inside were still folded, and he reached in and stirred them around. When he looked up at her again, she was smiling at him, making it hard for him to breathe.

"I'm glad I ran into you," Lilly said. "I wanted to apologize for the other night on the pier. You caught me on a bad day. All that talk about karma and the rest of it, I don't know where that came from."

"I didn't mind."

"You're sweet, but I'm not usually such a sad sack, especially around strangers."

Thomas started to tell her that she didn't seem like a stranger to him, but he thought better of it. Instead, he watched her as she turned back to the washing machine and her coins.

Eventually Lilly noticed he wasn't moving, and she motioned toward the empty machine two down from hers. "That one's open."

"What?"

"Your clothes," she said. "I've got these two, but I'm not using that one."

"Oh, right. Thanks."

Thomas adjusted the box in his arms and carried it to the open machine. As he passed behind her, he saw a dark-purple bruise on her arm, just above her elbow.

"That looks painful."

"What?"

"Your arm." He pointed. "I saw him grab you."

Lilly frowned and tried to pull her sleeve down to cover it. "It's nothing," she said. "I bruise so easily. If I so much as bump into something, I look like I've been in a car wreck the next day."

Thomas nodded and opened the lid of the washing machine. He dumped his clothes inside and set the empty box on the floor. Next to him, Lilly put the last of her coins into her machine, then turned to face him.

"I was going to come see you later."

Thomas's pulse quickened. "You were?"

"The light switch in my kitchen sparks every time I turn it on. I'm worried I'm going to electrocute myself one of these days, and I was hoping—"

"I can take a look."

Lilly smiled. "I left a message with the main office last week, but they haven't called me back. Do you think it's something you could fix?"

"The wires are probably loose," he said. "Should be easy."

"You're a lifesaver."

"I can look at it now if you'd like. I'm not doing anything."

There was a white clock mounted behind a rusted metal cage on the wall. Lilly glanced up at it, shook her head. "Not today. Mike won't be gone long, unless he stops at the Royale." She paused. "I don't want him to know I had someone else fix it."

"The Royale?"

"The bar at the end of the boardwalk, down by the arcade."

"And Mike is your husband?"

She nodded. "How about tomorrow morning? I don't know what your day looks like, but I'm free any—"

"I can do it tomorrow."

The words came out fast, too fast, and Lilly laughed under her breath.

Thomas bit down hard on the insides of his cheeks, silently cursing himself for being so eager. The next time he spoke, he fought to keep his voice slow and even.

"I mean, if tomorrow works for you."

"Just make sure Mike's car is gone," she said. "It's the blue one."

"I've seen it."

She smiled and turned back to the washing machine.

Thomas watched as she adjusted the settings, then pushed the coin tray in.

The coins dropped, and the water hissed. She closed the lid.

"I'll see you tomorrow morning," she said. "Thanks for helping, and sorry again about the other night on the pier."

"Nothing to be sorry about."

Lilly rolled her eyes and picked up her empty laundry basket. She balanced the basket on her hip and walked out.

Once the door closed behind her, Thomas leaned against the machine and exhaled, feeling the tension drain away. His mind was spinning, and the muscles in his legs trembled under his weight, but he couldn't stop smiling.

It'd worked.

He'd talked to her, and they'd connected.

She'd even invited him to her home.

Thomas took his clothes from the washer and dropped them back into the cardboard box. He was still smiling and still thinking about tomorrow as he lifted the box and headed toward the door.

When he passed Lilly's machine, he stopped.

He stood for a moment, listening to the water run. Then he stepped closer, opened the lid, and looked down at Lilly's clothes inside. The ones on top were still dry.

Slowly, he reached in, running his hands over her clothes, feeling the softness of the fabric, and imagining the softness of her. Then, his fingers touched something lacy and delicate, and his breath caught in his throat.

He removed a thin pair of black panties.

Thomas made a low noise in the back of his throat as he ran his fingers over the silk and lace, and for a time the room around him seemed to disappear.

When he snapped back, he looked around, then quickly slid the panties into the front pocket of his jeans before closing the lid of the machine. Then he took a slow, deep breath, adjusted his hold on the cardboard box, and hurried out of the laundry room.

As he walked back to his apartment, he couldn't bring himself to look up at Lilly's window. His heart was beating so hard that his chest ached, and every step he took seemed heavier than the last. He knew if he saw her now, she would read the guilt on his face like a confession, and she would know what he'd done.

Then again, maybe she wouldn't mind.

The thought both thrilled and terrified him, and by the time he got inside his apartment and locked the door behind him, his cheeks ached from smiling.

Chapter Five

The next morning Thomas woke up early. He waited by the window until he saw Mike leave the apartment, then he took his toolbox from under the bed and checked the clock on the nightstand.

Ten minutes to nine.

He sat down hard on the bed, rocking back and forth, his fingers tapping rapidly against his knees. When he couldn't sit any longer, he got up and paced back and forth through his apartment, moving from the kitchen at one end to the bathroom at the other, one eye always on the clock. When the numbers blinked 9:00, Thomas picked up the toolbox, but he forced himself to stand at the door, one hand on the doorknob, for two more minutes before walking out.

Outside, the sun was bright, and there was a cool breeze coming up from the ocean that chilled his skin as he crossed the parking lot and climbed the steps to Lilly's apartment.

He waited outside her door, switched the toolbox from one hand to the other, and then knocked three times, soft and unthreatening.

"You can do this," he whispered.

When Lilly opened the door, Thomas had to bite the insides of his cheeks to keep from sighing. She was wearing a thin blue sundress that fell over her like a shadow, hinting at the curves of her body like an unspoken promise.

It was almost too much, and he turned away.

He knew, at that moment, that if he looked at her, if he saw her smile, a part of him would die at her feet.

"Everything okay?" she asked.

"Fine." Thomas cleared his throat and turned back slowly. "You look nice."

Nice.

He regretted the word as soon as it was out of his mouth, but Lilly didn't seem to mind. She had a necklace with a silver key pendant around her neck, and she held it between two fingers, sliding the key back and forth along the chain.

She didn't say anything.

Thomas thought about apologizing, but before he could, she stepped back from the door and welcomed him inside.

"Thank you again," she said. "I hope this isn't too much trouble."

Thomas swallowed hard. "Happy to help."

Lilly's apartment was larger than his, and he waited just inside the door, taking it all in. The furniture, old and unmatched, looked comfortable in a lived-in way. There was a bloodred blanket draped over the back of the couch, and several different-colored throw pillows stacked against the cushions. A tower of library books stood balanced on the coffee table next to a worn sketch pad and several drawing pencils, and along the walls were an assortment of framed black-and-white photographs.

"The switch is in the kitchen," Lilly said. "I'll show you."

The kitchen was just off the living room, and Thomas followed her, glancing at a few of the photographs that hung along the wall as they went. "Are you a photographer?"

"Sometimes," she said. "I stopped after we moved here."

"You're good."

"Do you think so?"

"I do." Thomas stepped closer to one of the photos. In it, a man with a woman on either arm stood smiling in front of a line of towering red rocks. Behind them, blue snowcapped mountains shone in the distance. "Where was this taken?"

"Colorado Springs." She leaned in, pointed at the photo. "That's me and my sister with my dad, a few weeks before he died."

"You're a twin?"

"I am."

Thomas studied the photo, then pointed to one of the women. "That's you."

"How could you—" Lilly paused, eyes wide. "No one but my dad could ever tell us apart that quickly. Even he'd get it wrong sometimes."

"It's the smile. Yours is more . . ." He hesitated, searching for the word. "Kind."

"I'm impressed." She turned back to the photo, and Thomas thought he saw sadness in her eyes. "Her name's Maggie. She's nine minutes younger."

"Where does she live?"

"As far as I know, she's still in Manitou, but I couldn't tell you for sure. I haven't talked to her in over a year."

"You're not close?"

"Not at the moment," she said.

"Why not?"

Lilly laughed. "Aren't you a curious one?"

Thomas felt the blood rush to his face, and he stumbled over his words, trying to backtrack. "I'm sorry, I shouldn't be so nosy. I just—"

"No," Lilly said, laughing. "It's fine. But I don't think you want to hear about my family drama."

"I do if you want to tell me."

She seemed to consider him for a moment, then said, "It's a pretty dull story, to be honest. It might bore you."

He thought about telling her he wanted to know everything there was to know about her, but instead he said, "I like hearing other people's stories. It helps me get to know them. We are neighbors, after all."

"That's true."

"So," Thomas said. "You and your sister?"

"Where to begin . . ." Lilly hesitated. "Things started to go bad when I met Mike."

"She didn't like him?"

"That's putting it mildly," she said. "But maybe that's not fair to her. I think she tried to like him. They just have different personalities. Maggie is a creature of habit. She doesn't like change, so when things started getting serious with me and Mike, she didn't respond well."

"She wasn't happy for you?"

Lilly seemed to think about this for a moment, then said, "She wanted to be, but it was a tough time for both of us. Our father had just been killed, and Mike always being around pushed things over the edge. They were at each other's throats a lot."

"Your dad was killed?"

Lilly nodded. "He was a cop. Wrong place, wrong time."

Thomas thought she wanted to say more, but he could tell it wasn't easy for her, so he didn't push. Instead, he said, "How about your mother?"

"She died when we were little. I barely remember her." Lilly stood back, straightened her dress, her hand absently going to the key around her neck. "Every family has their own little tragedies, don't they? You really don't need to listen to mine."

"I don't mind," Thomas said. "I've never met a twin. Are you two alike?"

"In a lot of ways," she said. "But dig a little deeper and we're about as different as you can be."

"How so?"

Lilly laughed, shook her head. "Let's just say that Maggie likes rules. She likes when life follows a routine, and when things make sense. She doesn't like surprises, or any kind of disruption, and she doesn't do anything without thinking it through."

"And you're not like that?"

Lilly shrugged. "Life is short, you know what I mean?"

Thomas nodded. "Do you miss her?"

"Every single day." She glanced at the photo. "Some days are better than others, but most of the time it feels like I'm missing a piece of myself. She was my best friend my entire life. We were inseparable."

"Why don't you call her?"

Lilly shook her head. "I wrote her a letter last Christmas, trying to patch things up, but she never wrote me back."

"Maybe she didn't get it."

Lilly looked over at him, and this time the sadness in her eyes was unmistakable.

"Yeah," she said. "Maybe."

"If you called her, I bet—"

"I can't do that, Thomas," she said. "Too much has happened."

He started to ask why, but the tone of her voice stopped him. Whatever the history was between Lilly and her sister, he could tell he'd already taken the questions too far, and it was something best left alone.

So he let it drop.

"Do you want to show me that switch?" he asked. "I bet it's a loose wire."

"Is that hard to fix?"

"Not if you have a screwdriver," Thomas said, holding up the toolbox.

Lilly smiled and motioned for him to follow.

As they walked, Thomas watched the liquid sway of her hips as she led him into the kitchen, and he congratulated himself for playing things just right.

Everything had gone perfectly, even better than he'd hoped.

He'd listened to her story, asked questions, shown an interest in her life. But most importantly, he'd made her comfortable. It was obvious to him now that the sparks he'd felt between them that first night on the pier hadn't been in his imagination. They had a genuine connection, one as real as the stars in the sky.

Best of all, he thought she felt it, too.

For the first time, Thomas allowed himself to think about the future, their future, and he let his thoughts run free, exploring all the beautiful possibilities yet to come.

In some ways, it seemed almost too good to be true.

Chapter Six

Lilly stopped in the middle of the kitchen and pointed to the light switch on the wall beside the stove. "There she is."

"Breaker box?"

"In here." She opened a door beside the refrigerator, revealing a small silver panel mounted inside. "They're not marked, so you'll have to try a few."

Thomas set the toolbox on the ground, flipped the latches, and opened the lid. He took the screwdriver he needed, then flipped a couple of breakers until he found the right one. Once the power was off, he began unscrewing the plate.

"How long has this been going on?" he asked.

"Since we moved in. I tried to get Mike to fix it, but he's had a lot on his mind."

"Don't worry," Thomas said. "You can always count on me."

"Thanks." She took a pack of cigarettes from the counter, then sat at the kitchen table, watching him. "Speaking of Mike, can I ask you a favor?"

"Of course."

"If you run into him, I'd appreciate it if you didn't tell him you were here."

"You don't want him to know?"

"Do you mind?"

"I can keep a secret." The words sent a delicious chill down his spine, and Thomas smiled inside as he removed the switch from the wall. "If it were me, I wouldn't like knowing you were alone with another man while I was gone either."

Lilly didn't say anything, and it took a moment before Thomas noticed the silence. His words echoed back to him in his mind, and he felt his stomach drop. "I'm sorry, I didn't mean anything by that. I was only—"

"It's okay." She took a cigarette from the pack and lit it. "I don't usually keep secrets from Mike. It's just that sometimes he can be . . . sensitive about things."

"I understand."

"He's very good with his hands," she said. "He can fix anything, but he gets distracted, and he might not understand why I asked you for help. We don't always communicate very well."

"I won't say a word. I promise."

"Thank you." Lilly tapped her cigarette over a green glass ashtray and said, "So, your turn."

"My turn?"

"I've told you about me and my drama, so now it's your turn. Tell me your secrets. I'm feeling a little vulnerable."

"There's nothing to tell."

"Don't do that," she said. "We're neighbors, after all. Right?"

Thomas smiled. "What do you want to know?"

"Tell me about your family," Lilly said. "All I know is that you used to vacation at the Cove as a kid, and that your family owns my apartment."

"That's about all of it."

"Are you close with your folks?"

"They died almost ten years ago."

"Oh Christ," she said. "Me and my mouth."

"It's all right," he said. "There was a fire. They were asleep, never woke up."

"Were you there?"

Thomas began tightening the wires on the switch. "I was, but I got out."

"How old were you?"

"Fourteen."

"That must've been tough."

Thomas nodded, wanting to stop talking. The old tension was building inside of him, pulling him down. He tried to separate himself from the memory, grounding himself in the moment, the way he'd been taught.

It helped, but only a little.

He focused on the light switch, said, "I don't think about them too often."

"Really? I think about my dad all the time. We weren't prepared to lose him." She paused. "I think the finality of it is the worst. It sneaks up on you."

"Only if you let it."

Lilly didn't say anything, and when Thomas looked back at her, she was staring down at her cigarette and the thin ribbon of smoke unraveling into the air. He watched her for a moment, then asked, "Feeling less vulnerable?"

"Not really." She crushed her cigarette in the ashtray. "Maybe we should change the subject, talk about something prettier."

"Sure." Thomas dropped the screwdriver back in the toolbox and pushed himself to his feet. He opened the breaker box, turned the power on, and then flipped the light switch a couple of times, on and off. "No more sparks. Looks like I'm done here."

"Thank you so much."

"My pleasure." Thomas smiled at her. "Listen, have you eaten? I was thinking about walking down to the boardwalk. If you want to come along, we could grab breakfast and sit on the pier. I bet we can find something prettier to talk about."

Lilly looked up at him, a thin smile on her lips. "You're sweet, and thank you, but I'm not hungry."

"How about just the walk? We can get some fresh air." He motioned toward the door. "There's a fortune-teller down there I've been meaning to visit."

"You want to go see the witch?"

"I know. She's for tourists."

"Ah," she said. "A nonbeliever?"

"You're not?"

"Not anymore."

"What changed your mind?"

"This place changed my mind," she said. "I've seen too many weird things in this town not to wonder."

"Then what do you say?" He stepped closer and, without thinking, held out his hand to her. "It'll be fun, just the two of us."

Lilly stared at his hand, but she didn't take it, and when she looked up at him, her eyes had turned cold. "I appreciate the offer, Thomas, but it's not a good idea."

Thomas let his hand drop, feeling a rush of embarrassment. He started to ask if she wouldn't go because she was scared of her husband finding out, but he thought he already knew the answer, and he didn't want to hear her say it. Instead, he tried his best to smile. "Maybe another time?"

"Maybe," she said.

To Thomas, that was as good as a promise.

Lilly stood, and Thomas picked up the toolbox and followed her to the living room. Neither of them said anything else, and when Lilly opened the front door, she leaned against it, holding it open.

"Thank you again. I feel safer already."

"Anything you need." He stepped out, pausing just outside the door, then turned back to her. "I hope I didn't upset you."

"You didn't."

"It's just that I like talking to you," he said. "I didn't mean anything."

Lilly reached out and put her hand on his arm, and for an instant Thomas was overwhelmed by the urge to lean in and kiss her. The desire was so strong that he wasn't sure he'd be able to stop himself, but then he noticed she wasn't looking at him. She was focused on something over his shoulder, and she was frowning.

"Looks like you have a visitor," she said.

Thomas turned and saw a sheriff's cruiser parked in front of his apartment. Sheriff Parks was standing outside his door talking to a man in a gray suit. The man was holding a yellow legal pad.

"Looks serious."

Thomas barely heard her.

"Do you know what they want?" she asked.

"How would I know what they want?" There was an edge to his voice, and he bit down on the words. "I haven't talked to them yet."

"I guess that's true."

"It's probably nothing."

"I'll let you go find out," she said, stepping back. "Thanks again for helping. I'm sure I'll see you around."

As she started to close the door, Thomas realized she was slipping away from him, and he couldn't do anything to stop it. There was so much left to say, so many things to discover about her. He needed more time, and he tried desperately to think of the words that would keep her there, but he couldn't focus.

All he could think about were the two men waiting for him outside his apartment.

Then the door shut, the lock clicked into place, and Lilly was gone.

Chapter Seven

Thomas walked slowly down the stairs, and as he crossed the parking lot, it felt as if the world around him had changed. The sun seemed too bright, and the wind coming up from the ocean smelled sour. The joy he'd felt earlier was gone, replaced by regret and disappointment. The two men standing outside his apartment looked up at him as he approached. The sheriff nodded a greeting while the man in the gray suit frowned, took a pen from his breast pocket, and began writing on the yellow notepad.

"Morning, Tom," Sheriff Parks said. "Enjoying the day?"

Thomas didn't say anything. He looked from Parks to the man in the gray suit, still writing on the yellow pad.

The sheriff paused, said, "This is Dr. Riley from social services. He's been assigned to your case. We thought we'd come by and check in on you."

Dr. Riley stopped writing, lowered the yellow pad, and stared at Thomas. "We missed you at your appointment last week, Mr. Bennett."

Thomas did his best to stay calm. "I must've forgotten. Sorry."

Dr. Riley glanced at the sheriff, and something unsaid passed between them. Then he looked back to Thomas. "These appointments are mandatory. There's no leeway. If you don't attend—"

"It won't happen again."

Sheriff Parks stepped away from the door. "Dr. Riley needs to have a peek at your place for his report. Mind inviting us inside?"

Thomas knew the game, knew what was expected of him, and it was almost frightening how easy it was to slip back into the role he needed to play.

"Of course." He moved between the two men and unlocked his front door. As he stepped inside he said, "It's a studio apartment, so there's not a lot to see."

"Are you happy here?"

"I don't need much."

The two men followed him in. Dr. Riley looked around briefly, then made a note on the yellow pad. "Tell me about your daily routine."

Thomas barely heard him. His thoughts kept drifting back to Lilly, making it hard to focus. The look he'd seen on her face as she closed the door on him was seared into his mind, and he wondered if she was having second thoughts about him. He tried to think of what he could have done differently, because he'd been so close, so very close—

"Mr. Bennett?"

Thomas snapped back. "Sorry," he said. "What do you need to know?"

"Your routine," Dr. Riley said. "What time you get up in the morning, what you do, where you go, who you interact with, that kind of thing."

Thomas explained his job, how he was responsible for the daily upkeep and basic maintenance of the apartments. He told them he rarely saw anyone, and that he hadn't had time to go anywhere, other than the occasional walk along the boardwalk, and that most of his time lately had been spent cleaning up after the storm.

"That was a rough one," Sheriff Parks said. "We lost power for two days."

Dr. Riley didn't speak. His attention remained on Thomas.

"We didn't lose power out here," Thomas said. "But I'm still cleaning all the debris left behind. It should keep me busy for a while."

"Was that what you were doing when we arrived?"

"No, I was fixing a light switch for a tenant."

"Do you have many tenants?"

"Just one," Thomas said. "Well, two, I guess, but they're in the same apartment."

"No one else?"

"No one else."

"That must leave you with a lot of free time." Dr. Riley flipped a page in the notepad. "Has that been a problem?"

"Having free time?"

Dr. Riley looked up from the notepad, stared at him, silent.

"Like I said, I haven't had much free time."

"Not yet, at least." Dr. Riley made another note. "Have you spoken to anyone back home?"

"Why would I do that?"

"I thought you might have friends there."

"I don't," Thomas said, trying to keep the edge out of his voice. "And this is my home now."

"Of course," Dr. Riley said. "I just thought you might be—"

"There's no one there I'd want to talk to."

"Clean slate," Sheriff Parks said. "I can understand that."

Dr. Riley frowned, but he didn't break his gaze with Thomas.

"Is that strange?" Thomas asked. "Wanting to start over?"

"Not at all," Dr. Riley said. "My concern would be an unwillingness to accept what happened. If your reluctance stems from denying the events that took place there, I'd want to know why."

"I'm not denying anything."

"I'm not saying that you are, only that it's a legitimate concern."

"I'm not denying anything."

Dr. Riley closed the notepad and held it against his chest. "Have you made your tenants aware of your history?"

"Why would I do that?"

"Full disclosure."

Thomas tried to imagine what Lilly would think of him if she knew, and the thought made his chest burn. "Those records are sealed."

"So you have no intention of telling them?"

"It's none of their business." Thomas turned to Sheriff Parks. "Those records are sealed. I was a juvenile, and I was confused. I'm not the person I was back then, and I don't want anyone to judge me for things I—"

"It's okay, Tom," the sheriff said. "Those records are sealed, and you don't have to tell anyone about what happened if you don't want to. Isn't that right, Doc?"

Dr. Riley nodded.

"Then why are you asking me about it?" Thomas could hear the tension rising in his voice, but it was beyond his control. "Why are you pushing me? Would you go around telling everyone if you were me?"

"Thomas." Dr. Riley's voice was irritatingly calm. "You're completely within your rights to live your life however you see fit. There are no right or wrong answers to any of my questions. I'm only interested in the reasoning behind your decisions."

Thomas didn't say anything, and for a moment they were all quiet.

Sheriff Parks moved toward the window and leaned down to look out. "You know, you won't have much free time come spring. This place books up fast during the season."

"I remember."

Parks turned back to him. "That's right, you know all about the summers here."

Thomas nodded.

"Does that worry you?" Dr. Riley asked. "Having so many people around?"

"Not at all," Thomas said, and it was the truth. He wasn't looking forward to the tourists, but they didn't worry him either. The solitude of the off-season was one of the reasons he'd been excited to come to Beaumont Cove, and four months of crowds was a small price to pay for eight months of solitude. "It's only for the summer."

"I can tell you I'm not looking forward to it," Parks said, laughing. "That's my busiest time of the year. Tourists are a handful."

"I'll be fine." Thomas stared at Dr. Riley. "And I'll call to set up a new appointment this week."

"That won't be necessary." Dr. Riley took a card from his jacket pocket, turned it over on the notepad, and wrote on the back. "I'll mark this visit down as the appointment you missed, but I want to see you in my office next month."

"Next month?"

Dr. Riley handed the card to Thomas. "You can call to set the date. I wrote my schedule on the back."

Thomas looked down at the card, the blue ink, the sharp, arrogant writing. "Thanks," he said. "I'll call this week."

"Good." Dr. Riley nodded to Parks and moved toward the door. "I look forward to following your progress, Thomas. You seem to be off to a promising start."

Thomas watched them as they walked back to the cruiser. Once they were gone, he closed the door and sat on the edge of his bed. He could feel the tension inside of him slowly draining away, like a bitter aftertaste. The past few weeks on his own, with no one to answer to, had spoiled him, and he'd foolishly believed his days of having to maneuver around doctors and bureaucrats were behind him.

Now he wondered if it would ever really be over.

He leaned back on the bed and closed his eyes.

The day had started out so well, and he tried to return to how he'd felt that morning with Lilly, before the sheriff had shown up and everything had gone wrong.

He tried telling himself that it wasn't as bad as he thought.

Things might not have turned out perfectly with Lilly, but nothing was ruined. They'd had a good time together, laughing and talking. She had confided in him, after all, and that counted for something. In a way, he felt as though their bond was even stronger now than it'd been before.

She just needed time, and he needed to be patient.

Thomas pushed himself up, leaning on his elbow, and pulled Lilly's black panties out from under his pillow. He lay back on the bed and ran his fingers over the fabric, clearing his mind of all thoughts and worries, focusing only on her.

He thought of the blue dress she wore that morning, and the way she'd played with the key on her necklace as her eyes met his. He remembered how badly he'd wanted to kiss her, how deep that desire had been.

But he'd been a coward.

Thomas unbuckled his belt and pushed his pants down around his thighs. He pressed the lacy black fabric to his nose and inhaled deeply, breathing in her scent and her secrets. He could almost hear her voice in his ear, whispering to him as he slid her panties over his face and down his chest, imagining the feel of her skin against his, her hand moving lower, wrapping around him, tight and divine, until there was only her.

And when he came, he wept.

Chapter Eight

Magnolia

We followed the medical examiner back to his office. He dropped the clipboard on his desk and opened the top drawer. There was a small manila envelope inside. He took it out and handed it to me.

"These are the personal items she was wearing when they brought her in."

I opened the flap on the envelope and turned it over, letting the contents slide out into my palm. Inside were two silver stud earrings, a black bracelet, and a thin gold wedding ring.

"Is this it?" I asked. "There should be a necklace with a silver key."

"If it's not there, she wasn't wearing it."

I looked down at the items in my hand, frowned, then put everything back into the envelope and dropped it into the wastebasket beside the desk. Parks stared at me, and I saw the confusion in his eyes, but I ignored it. The medical examiner either didn't notice or he didn't care. He crossed the room to a filing cabinet, opened the drawer, and began gathering papers.

"There are a few forms you'll need to sign."

It was more than a few, and when we finally finished the paperwork, Sheriff Parks led me out of the hospital and back into the rain. As we walked to the cruiser, all I could think about was Lilly.

The official cause of death was asphyxiation, but the deep finger-sized bruises around her throat were only part of what Mike had done to her. When Lilly died she had four broken ribs, a fractured cheekbone, a dislocated jaw, and a series of fresh bruises on top of older bruises that had never had a chance to heal.

The list went on.

"I'll take you to the hotel," Parks said. "Get you settled in."

I nodded, but I didn't feel like talking, and Sheriff Parks seemed to understand. It wasn't until we were on the road and heading back to town that he spoke.

"I met your sister once," he said. "She came into the office last spring. She seemed nice."

"Why was she there?"

"She wanted to dispute a drunk and disorderly ticket I gave her husband." He made a soft scoffing sound. "Now Mike I got to know well."

"I'm not surprised."

Parks smiled a sad smile, then sat up in his seat, eyes focused on the road ahead. I could tell he was steadying himself to say something, but I wasn't sure I wanted to hear it. The day had been heavy enough, and I didn't know if I could take much more. I tried to think of something to say that might change the conversation before it started, but I couldn't, and then it was too late.

"I should've seen the signs," he said. "If I'd paid closer attention, I might've been able to help."

"It wouldn't have mattered."

"Maybe not," he said. "But I could've tried harder, and I didn't."

"That makes two of us." I turned to face him. "Can I ask you something?"

"Anything."

"Were you the one who arrested Mike that night?"

Parks shook his head. "One of my deputies picked him up, but I was on duty when the call came in, and I saw him later that night."

"Did he say why he did it?"

"No, but he'd been drinking."

"How did he act?"

"Confused," Parks said. "They always play dumb at first, but once they know we have them, that changes."

"He didn't try to tell you his side of things?"

Sheriff Parks glanced over at me and then back at the road. "All he kept saying was that he didn't do it, and that she was fine when he left."

"Of course."

I thought about the first time Lilly had come home with a fist-sized bruise on the side of her face. I knew what'd happened, and when I confronted her, she didn't deny it. All she did was insist that it wasn't a problem, and that it was just a misunderstanding. It wasn't until I grabbed my keys and tried to go after him that she got upset and begged me to leave it alone.

Mike always had an excuse, and like a fool, she always believed him.

That was the biggest fight Lilly and I had ever been in, and it never ended. From that day on, I refused to have anything to do with Mike, and I tried again and again to convince her that she was making a mistake, but she wouldn't listen. She told me it was her life, and if she was making a mistake, it was hers to make.

She told me she could handle him.

And like a fool, I believed her.

"I want to see him."

Parks nodded. "I'll arrange it."

"Today."

"Today?"

"Right now."

Parks didn't say anything, and I could tell he was going over the idea in his head, looking for a way out. "Miss James, I'm not sure that's a good idea."

"Didn't you say you wanted to help in any way you could?"

"I believe I am helping you."

"By not helping me?"

"By saying I don't think it's a good idea." He paused. "I understand that you need closure, but hasn't the day been emotional enough? I can set something up for tomorrow or the next day, but I promise that seeing him now isn't going to make you feel better."

"I don't want to feel better," I said. "And no offense, but I'm not staying in this town any longer than I have to. I plan on being on the first bus out of here, but I can't do that until I see him."

"How about early tomorrow?"

"How about today?"

Parks exhaled slowly. "You'll be less emotional after a full night's sleep."

I laughed out loud. "Sheriff, I can't remember the last time I had a full night's sleep, and as far as my emotions go, I'm afraid this is as good as it ever gets." I turned in my seat, facing him as he drove. "I need to see him today. Please."

Sheriff Parks leaned back, sinking into the driver's seat. He tapped his thumb on the steering wheel, then said, "I'll have to radio ahead so they know we're coming."

"Thank you."

"He might not want to see you. Have you thought about that?" Parks frowned. "If I were him, I wouldn't want to see you, especially after what he did."

"He'll see me."

"How do you know that?"

"Because we're family."

Chapter Nine

Thomas

It was late, and Thomas had just fallen asleep when someone knocked at his door. At first he thought the sound was part of a dream, and he stayed in bed. Then the knock came again, louder, more insistent, and Thomas sat up. His pants were folded over the back of the chair, and he stepped into them as he crossed the room.

He stopped at the door, said, "Who is it?"

"Open the door, Thomas."

It was a man's voice, and one he didn't recognize. Thomas unlocked the latch and inched the door open. Mike was standing outside. Thomas had seen him only from a distance, and he was surprised at how big he was up close.

Slowly, Thomas pulled the door open, trying to stand as straight as he could.

Mike had his hands in his pockets, and he didn't say anything right away. Instead, he just stood staring, a half smile on his face.

"You're Thomas?" The smile grew. "You?"

"Can I help you with something?"

Mike took his hands from his pockets and leaned against the doorframe. The movement was quick, and Thomas stepped back. Mike noticed, and his smile widened, splitting across his face like a wound.

"You seem a little jumpy."

Thomas smelled alcohol on his breath.

"I'm Mike." He held out his hand. Thomas looked at it for a moment before taking it. "I thought I'd introduce myself since it seems you already met my wife."

"Lilly," he said. "Yeah, we met on the pier."

"That's right. She told me that was you." Mike's grip was strong, and he held the handshake. "Hard to keep up. You all look the same to me."

Thomas tried to take his hand back, but Mike squeezed his fingers, hard, making him wince before letting go.

"That's the problem with having a beautiful wife. There are always guys like you lurking around, trying to worm their way in."

Thomas shook his head. "You've got the wrong idea."

"Do I?" Mike smiled. "Because I know how Lilly can be. That's why I'm here. I thought if I explained the situation, I could save you some pain in the future."

"Nothing happened."

Mike laughed. "I know that," he said. "I'm only concerned about you."

"Me?"

"You see, Lilly collects admirers," he said. "Half the time she doesn't realize she's doing it. It's just her nature to gather strays. The trouble is, every now and then one of you strays gets the wrong idea, and then it becomes my problem to handle."

"There's no problem," Thomas said.

"I'm glad to hear it." Mike glanced back at his apartment, hesitated. "Look, Thomas, you seem harmless enough, and I'd hate for this to become an issue. I don't need the hassle, and you don't need that kind of attention. Do you agree?"

Thomas nodded.

"Good." Mike reached in and put his hand on Thomas's shoulder and squeezed. "From now on, how about letting me take care of any repairs in my apartment. That way you can focus on other things around here and keep yourself out of trouble."

"It's my job to—"

"Thomas." There was an edge to Mike's voice, and Thomas stopped talking. "I'm trying to help you. The path you're walking is a dangerous one. If you don't listen to me, it's going to lead you somewhere you really don't want to go. Are we clear?"

Thomas paused. "We're clear."

"Good." Mike's face seemed to soften, but his eyes stayed hard and focused. "I'm glad to hear it." He let go of Thomas's shoulder and stepped back from the door. "Now, I've got to go and have a talk with Lilly. Sleep well, Thomas."

Mike started back across the parking lot, and Thomas closed the door, his heart beating fast. The clock on the nightstand read 3:15 a.m., and Thomas stared at the neon-red numbers, thinking about what Mike had said, and knowing he wasn't going to get back to sleep anytime soon.

He couldn't understand how a woman as perfect as Lilly could lower herself to marry a man like Mike. He knew there were women who stayed with men like that even though they knew better, but he never would've believed Lilly could be one of them.

It didn't make sense. She had to know she could do better.

Maybe he could show her.

Maybe he could be her way out.

Thomas went to the kitchen and made a pot of coffee. While it brewed, he sat at the table and turned on the radio. The classical station was playing Beethoven. Not his favorite, but it seemed to fit his mood. He decided the next time he saw Lilly, he would tell her how he felt, so there would be no misunderstanding.

He would show her his heart.

Thomas wondered what she would say and where his confession would lead. Once she understood how he felt about her, would she tell him she felt the same way? Would she fall into his arms and give herself over to him, lips parted, soul exposed?

Thomas shuddered with pleasure at the thought.

It was past noon when Mike hurried to his car and sped out of the parking lot.

Thomas was on a ladder outside building two, fixing a gutter that had come loose during the storm, and he watched as the El Camino turned onto Main Street and roared toward town. He listened as the sound of the engine faded, then climbed down the ladder and crossed the parking lot to Lilly's apartment.

Her curtains were drawn, and there was no noise coming from inside.

He knocked, waited.

No one answered.

He knocked again, louder. "Lilly?"

This time he heard movement inside, and a shadow passed behind the peephole. He smiled, but then the shadow moved away and the door stayed closed.

Thomas leaned close. "I thought I'd check and see if you were okay. If you don't want to talk, I can come back later, I just—"

He heard the lock click and he stepped back. The door opened a few inches, and Lilly looked out at him through the crack.

"Hey," he said. "Is everything okay?"

"You shouldn't be here, Thomas," Lilly said. "Mike will be back. If he sees you—"

"He came to my apartment last night."

"I know."

"He was upset."

"I know."

"I was worried about you."

"Thomas." Lilly's voice sounded tired. "You should stay away from us. You don't want to be involved in this."

"If I got you into trouble, I'll talk to him and tell him it was all me. You didn't—"

"No," Lilly said. "Don't say anything. I can handle Mike. He'll cool off after a while, he always does, and then everything will be fine."

"But—"

"Thomas, please," she said. "Stay out of it."

"I'm not scared of him."

Lilly looked up at him, a sad smile.

Thomas stared at her, unsure of what to say next. He'd prepared himself, and he was ready to tell her how he felt. He wanted to open his heart to her, ask her to leave with him, to run away before Mike returned. But before he could say the words that would change their lives forever, Lilly stepped away from the door, and Thomas caught a flash of a bruise along her cheek.

Without thinking, he reached out and pushed the door open, just enough to see her face.

Lilly tried to turn away, but it was too late. Even in the dim light of the apartment, he could see the angry swelling around her eye, the split lip, the darkening bruise along her cheek.

"He hit you?"

"Thomas, just go."

"He hit you." Thomas felt the tension building, and he fought to keep it under control. "Did you call the police?"

"Of course not," she said. "It's no big deal."

"He has no right to hit you." Thomas tried to keep his voice calm and failed. "You don't deserve that. You don't need to be with some asshole who—"

"It's not like that," Lilly said. "He's under a lot of pressure, and I shouldn't have asked you to fix—"

"Leave him."

Lilly stopped. "What?"

Thomas paused.

This was his chance.

He would tell her everything, for better or worse.

The words were there, waiting for him to bring them into the world, to give them life. He was ready, and she was waiting, but when he opened his mouth to speak, all the words he'd dreamed of telling her ran from him.

Instead, he said. "What about your sister?"

Lilly frowned. "What about her?"

"You could go live with her," he said. "Get away from him."

"I won't do that," she said. "Even if I wanted to leave him, I couldn't call her."

"Then I'm going to say something to him."

"No you're not." Lilly spoke slowly. "You're going to leave it alone."

"I'm supposed to do nothing, knowing what he did to you?"

"You're supposed to mind your own business."

Lilly's voice was cold, and Thomas felt the words cut into him like a blade.

"I'm sorry you had to see this," she said. "And I'm sorry you're involved at all, but this has nothing to do with you. I like you, Thomas. You're kind, and you're gentle, and the world needs more gentle men, but this is my life, and I have it under control. It's none of your business."

Thomas stood there, locked and aching.

"Lilly, wait."

"Go home," she said, stepping back from the door. "Please."

Thomas watched the door close on him, and he didn't say a word.

Chapter Ten

Thomas unlocked the office door and hurried across the room toward the desk. He opened the top drawer and ran a finger down the list of emergency numbers taped inside, stopping at the main number for the sheriff's office. He read the numbers out loud and then picked up the phone, repeating them in a whisper as he dialed.

A woman answered on the second ring. "Sheriff's office."

The woman's voice sounded tired and indifferent, and it touched a shade of doubt forming in the back of Thomas's mind. What was he trying to do? He knew what would happen if he told the sheriff about what Mike had done. He knew they'd come out and talk to Lilly, see her bruises, and then put Mike in jail for a night. He also knew that Lilly wouldn't press charges, so Mike would go free, and it would all start again. Except this time, Lilly would see him as the bad guy, and she wouldn't want anything to do with him.

That was too high a price to pay.

"Sorry," Thomas said. "Wrong number."

The woman grunted and hung up.

Thomas kept the phone to his ear until the line clicked. Then he sank back in the chair, staring out over the shadowed office and the thin lines of sunlight leaking into the room through the blinds.

There was a Beaumont Cove snow globe sitting on the desk, and Thomas leaned forward and picked it up. He ran his thumb over the glass and smiled. Nearly every gift shop in town sold them, just another cheap souvenir for the tourists, but when he shook the globe and saw the tiny white flakes swirl around the miniature boardwalk and Ferris wheel, he lost himself in the scene.

Then his thoughts turned black.

By the time he noticed the shift, it was almost too late to stop the darkness from creeping into his mind. It'd come so suddenly, and with such desperation, that it terrified him, and he cursed himself for being so careless. He'd dropped his guard, and he'd let his thoughts seep into corners and crevices where he knew better than to go. It was shocking how easily it'd happened, and how eager the darkness was to return.

In the future, he would need to be more careful.

If he wanted Lilly, he'd have to keep his mind focused. Once she understood how he felt, and once she saw Mike for what he truly was, she would come to him. But first, he would have to prove to her that he could protect her.

He'd have to show her he was worthy of her love.

Thomas set the snow globe back on the desk, then got up and crossed the room to the windows at the front of the office. He split the blinds with two fingers and looked out at Main Street and the driveway leading into the empty parking lot. He wanted nothing more than to go back to Lilly's apartment and tell her not to worry, that he was going to take care of everything, and that she didn't need to be scared, but he couldn't. Lilly had made it clear that she didn't want him involved.

Except, he was involved.

As much as he wanted to respect her wishes, he wasn't going to stand by and let Mike hurt her anymore. He was going to protect her. Lilly might not like it, at least not at first, but that was the way it was going to be.

She didn't have a choice.

The sun was starting to set when the blue El Camino pulled into the parking lot and stopped in its normal spot at the foot of the steps leading up to Lilly's apartment.

Thomas was ready.

He stepped out of his apartment and moved steadily toward the car. He'd spent the afternoon going over everything he planned on saying to Mike until it felt natural. But as he approached the car, his mind was blank. He told himself not to worry, that it would all come back to him when the time came, and that the most important thing was that Lilly saw what he was doing for her.

He hoped she was watching.

Thomas heard the heavy pulse of bass coming from the speakers inside the car, vibrating the back window. The engine was still running, and he saw Mike sitting behind the wheel. At first he didn't understand why he wasn't getting out, but then Thomas noticed someone sitting in the passenger seat, and he stopped walking.

A warning light flashed in the back of Thomas's mind, and for a second he considered turning around and walking back to his apartment, but he couldn't. He was doing this for Lilly, and she needed him to be strong.

It was too late to run away.

Thomas stopped next to the driver's side and tapped on the window.

Mike had an open beer in his lap, and he was laughing with the person in the passenger seat, but when he turned and saw Thomas, his smile faded. Slowly, he reached down and shut off the engine, said something to the person next to him, then opened the door and got out, never taking his eyes off Thomas.

"What do you need, Thomas?"

The passenger door opened, and a skeleton of a man stepped out. He wore a black T-shirt, and his arms were covered in a collage of small tattoos that ran from his shoulders to his wrists. He had a thin, patchy beard, and there were dark circles under his eyes that looked almost black against his pale skin.

Thomas hadn't planned for him.

He'd wanted to talk to Mike alone, thought he knew how he would react, but an audience made things unpredictable, and Thomas's mind went blank.

"Spit it out," Mike said. "Something I can do for you?"

Thomas looked from Mike to the man on the passenger side and then back.

He had no words.

Mike laughed. "Good talk, champ." He reached out and clapped Thomas on the shoulder, then pushed past him and grabbed a case of beer out of the back end of the El Camino. He secured it under his arm and started toward the stairs.

The thin man followed.

Thomas felt his chance slipping away. He had to show Lilly what she meant to him, but he couldn't even speak. He glanced up at her window, saw the closed curtains, and thought of her inside, bruised and frightened and alone.

It was all he needed to find his voice.

"I know what you did to her."

Mike stopped halfway up the stairs and slowly turned around. He frowned, then tore open the case of beer and started back down to the parking lot.

He stopped in front of Thomas, and when he spoke, his voice was an edged whisper. "Is that really what you want to talk about?"

Thomas nodded.

"Okay, we can have that conversation, but not tonight. I have a guest." He reached into the case and took out one of the beer cans. "In the meantime, have a beer." He pushed the can into Thomas's chest, hard, knocking him back. "It's on me."

Mike turned and walked away, shaking his head.

"I want you to leave her alone."

"I said later, Thomas."

The thin man smiled at Mike, and when he got closer, he said something to him that Thomas couldn't hear, and they both laughed.

Thomas looked down at the blue-and-red can in his hand, feeling his muscles get tight and a slow burn of anger build in his chest. He was being dismissed, like he didn't matter, but the worst part was that they were laughing at him.

The slow burn in his chest grew hot.

Thomas stepped forward and threw the can as hard as he could. He watched as it left his hand, followed its arc as it tumbled through the air, and heard the dull thump it made when it struck the back of Mike's skull.

The sound of a hammer striking wet wood.

Mike dropped, falling forward on the steps. The case of beer slipped from under his arm, and several cans rolled out, cascading down the steps.

The thin man crouched next to Mike, who had his hand pressed against the back of his head, and yelled, "What the hell, man? Are you crazy?"

Thomas barely heard him.

He was looking up at Lilly's window, hoping.

Then he saw the curtains move and Lilly step in behind the glass. She looked down at him, and Thomas felt a sudden rush of joy knowing that she saw what he did for her, and that now she knew how far he'd go to keep her safe.

Things would be different now.

He was still staring up at her when he heard the thin man yell, "Mike, stop. It's not worth it."

Thomas turned back in time to see Mike coming toward him, fists clenched, eyes focused, a line of blood running along the side of his neck.

Thomas took a step back, but it was too late.

The first punch connected just below his left eye, snapping his head back. The power behind the blow shocked him, but there was no pain, just disorientation and a sudden, high-pitched ringing in his ears.

The next punch connected with the left side of Thomas's ribs, knocking the air from his lungs, and buckling his legs. Thomas dropped to one knee, struggling to breathe as a sea of black flowers bloomed behind his eyes.

The ringing in his ears turned into a scream.

Somewhere, far away, he thought he heard Lilly yelling, but he wasn't sure. Everything was happening so fast, and when he tried to look for her, all he saw was Mike and a steady blur of fists.

And then, only darkness.

Chapter Eleven

When Thomas opened his eyes, he was on his back, staring up at a gray sky streaked with orange. He could taste blood in his mouth, and when he tried to sit up, the ground fell away underneath him, and he slipped back down, leaning on one elbow. He tried again, but then he felt a hand on his shoulder, stopping him. The thin man was leaning over him, blocking the sky.

"Take it easy," the man said. "Don't get up too fast."

Thomas tried to speak, but the blood in his throat choked the words. He rolled to the side, coughed, and felt something hard rattle in his mouth.

He spit half of a broken tooth out onto the asphalt.

"What the hell were you thinking, man?"

Thomas slowly pushed himself up to sitting. He swallowed a mouthful of blood and felt his stomach cramp. For a second, he thought he was going to be sick, but then Lilly was next to him, leaning down, and the feeling passed.

"Is he okay?" she asked.

The thin man snickered, put a hand on Thomas's shoulder. "Well, he's not dead."

Thomas shrugged the hand away, then leaned forward, arms on knees, and looked up at Lilly. "I'm fine."

The thin man laughed under his breath, then stood and walked away, joining Mike by the stairs. Once he was gone, Lilly crouched next to Thomas and said, "You should go home, Thomas. Clean yourself up."

"Come with me."

"What?"

"Come with me," he repeated. "Can't you see what he is? You deserve better than him. I would never treat you like—"

"Stop." She glanced over her shoulder at Mike, and when she turned back, her eyes were wide and filled with fear. "Keep your voice down."

"He should know."

"Know what?"

"The truth."

"What truth?"

"The truth about us." Thomas leaned forward and slowly pushed himself to his feet. "We don't have to pretend anymore."

Lilly shushed him, then looked back at Mike. He was standing at the stairs, picking up the spilled beer cans, and ignoring them both. Then she turned to Thomas and hissed, "I don't know what you think is going on, but there is no us, and if he hears you, he'll—"

"I want him to hear me," he said. "I want him to know."

Lilly pressed her hands together in front of her mouth as if in prayer, then she turned her back on him and walked away. Thomas reached out to stop her, grabbing her arm, but she pulled away hard. "Don't touch me."

"He doesn't love you, not like I do."

"Thomas, shut up." He could hear the fear in her voice. "Please, go home."

"Not until you tell him about us."

"There is no us."

Then, behind her, Mike said, "What did he say?"

Lilly closed her eyes, and for an instant her entire body seemed to tremble.

Thomas reached for her. "Don't be scared," he said. "I won't let him hurt you."

Lilly backed away.

Mike moved closer. "What the hell is this, Lilly?"

"I—" She turned to him, but when she spoke, she stumbled over her words. "I don't know what he's talking about. He's crazy, I—"

"I'm not crazy," Thomas said. "I love you, and you love me."

Mike laughed out loud, then pushed past Lilly, moving toward Thomas. The thin man grabbed his arm, straining to pull him back. He turned to Thomas and said, "I suggest you walk away, right now."

Thomas barely heard him. He was staring at Lilly standing off to the side, wiping tears from her cheeks. When their eyes met, she looked away.

"Lilly, tell him," Thomas said. "Tell him that you—"

"Shut up!" She screamed at him. "I don't love you, and there's nothing between us. There's never been anything between us. You're insane."

For a second Thomas didn't know what to say. None of this had turned out the way he'd planned. Instead of being happy and grateful, Lilly was terrified, and the realization that it was all his fault stabbed into his chest like an ice pick, making it hard to breathe.

He wanted to understand, but it didn't make sense.

"Lilly, don't do this." He moved closer to her. "Don't throw this away."

"What is wrong with you?" The softness in her face was gone, replaced by sharp lines and angles. "I don't even know you."

Thomas felt the air around him grow cold.

She was slipping away from him, right in front of his eyes, and he couldn't stop it. He needed to bring her back to him, but he couldn't think clearly.

"Don't do this," he said. "You and me. We can still—"

Lilly pushed him, hard, and Thomas stumbled back, stunned and silent. Then she stepped closer. At first he thought she was going to push him again, but instead, she leaned in and whispered so only he could hear.

"You disgust me."

The anger and fear behind those words clawed into him, and he backed away from her. Mike and the thin man were standing behind her, watching him. He wanted to say something, anything, but when he tried to speak, all that came out was a soft moan.

Then they began to laugh.

Slowly, Thomas turned and walked away.

He could feel them watching him, and he focused on each step, willing himself not to stumble. Behind him, he heard Mike yelling at Lilly, but it all seemed so far away, and he barely noticed. The world had dulled around him, turned gray, and their voices slipped easily into the colorless haze.

But Lilly's words echoed in his mind.

You disgust me.

Thomas walked past his apartment, past the main office, and crossed over Main Street. He started down toward the boardwalk, past the closed gift shops and food stands lining the long path leading to the shore. A few people were out, and they turned to stare at his bruised and bloodied face as he passed, but he didn't care.

They didn't matter to him.

They didn't even exist.

They were ghosts.

He walked to the edge of the boardwalk and stopped at the railing and looked out over the water. The waves rolled in, gray and unrelenting, and Thomas stared at them for a while, then turned and scanned the beach.

In the distance, something large had washed up on the shore, and a blur of ocean birds danced around it like an angry fire. Thomas watched as they screamed and fought, clawing for a piece of the rotting mass.

Eventually he turned away and walked out onto the Starlight Pier.

It was high tide, and each new wave hitting the pier sent a cold spray of mist into the air. Thomas found the spot where he'd first seen Lilly. He didn't know what had brought him to this spot, only that it was important for him to remember a time when he'd made her smile.

To his right, an older couple stood, arm in arm, staring out at the sea. Thomas studied the way she pressed herself against him, the way she touched his arm. He wondered how they'd met, what he'd done to get her to look at him the way she did.

It all seemed so random, a roll of the dice.

Love or loneliness, written in the stars.

Eventually, the couple noticed him staring. They smiled politely, then moved a few steps down the railing, away from him. Thomas kept staring, and after a while the woman whispered something in the man's ear.

The man turned to Thomas, frowned. "Looks like you've had a bad day."

Thomas met his gaze, silent, then smiled. He felt the cut on his lip split open and a fresh line of blood run down his chin and drip onto his shirt.

The woman inhaled sharply and turned her back on Thomas. The man shook his head, frowned, and led her down the pier toward the boardwalk.

Thomas watched them go, then turned back to the sea.

He kept hearing Lilly's voice in his head, telling him he disgusted her, followed by Mike, laughing at him. Everything about what'd happened replayed itself in his mind, and the harder he tried to push it away, the louder and more vivid the memory became.

For a long time, he didn't know what to do.

Then, all at once, the answer came, hitting him so hard that he stepped back from the railing. The solution was so simple, so perfect, that when the pieces began to fall into place in his mind, he laughed out loud, and for a moment he lost himself in the beautiful balance of the universe.

He knew exactly what he had to do.

It was as if it'd been written in the stars.

Chapter Twelve

Magnolia

Sheriff Parks made the call, and a half hour later we were waved through the barbed wire–topped gates of the Beaumont County jail. The rain had finally stopped, but the gray clouds hung low and threatening in the sky. The anger I felt still burned inside of me, but I had it under control. Whatever happened when I saw him, whatever he said to me, I swore to myself that I'd stay calm.

We parked beside the front door, and I followed Sheriff Parks inside. He waited while I made my way through security, and then he led me to a waiting room with a television mounted on the wall, and several rows of empty folding chairs.

"Feel free to change the channel," he said. "I'll let them know we're here. Shouldn't be too long."

I sat on one of the chairs closest to the door and glanced up at the TV. On-screen, a woman sat crying in front of a studio audience while another woman with a microphone watched her with practiced sympathy. I got up and turned it off, then walked to the window and looked out past the fences toward the long fields filled with wild grass. In the distance, a line of sand-colored hills dotted with scrub rolled easily along the horizon.

Several minutes slipped by, and then Parks was back.

"You ready?"

I took a breath and followed him out of the waiting room and through a large metal door at the end of the hallway. He led me to a quiet room with three semiprivate cubicles split by glass. There was a mounted phone on the privacy wall of each cubicle, and the thick glass dividing the room was scratched and stained nicotine yellow.

I sat at the last cubicle in the line.

"Last time I'll ask," he said. "Are you sure about this?"

I told him I was.

"Then I'll leave you to it. They should bring him down in a minute." Sheriff Parks moved toward the door, stopped. "If you need anything, I'll be right outside."

I thanked him, then sat and watched the closed door on the other side of the glass.

Five minutes later, that door opened and a guard led Mike into the room. He was dressed in a standard orange jumpsuit, and his hands were cuffed in front of him. When he saw me, I thought I saw a flash of surprise on his face, but it was gone so quickly that I couldn't be sure. The guard guided him toward the chair across from me, and as he unlocked the cuffs, he said something to him that I couldn't hear through the glass.

Mike nodded and sat down.

We stared at each other through the glass until the guard moved away, then Mike reached for the phone on the wall beside him. I hesitated, wondering if I was as ready for this conversation as I'd thought, but knowing it was too late now.

I took a deep breath and reached for the phone.

"I didn't kill your sister."

Mike's voice was calm, but there was an edge of desperation buried behind the words. If I hadn't known him, I might not have picked up on it, but it was there, crystal clear, and hearing it almost made me smile.

Almost.

"She was fine when I left. She even—" He paused, noticing the look on my face. "All right, we had an argument, and I might've gotten a little carried away, but when I left that night, Lilly was fine."

I frowned.

"It wasn't like before," he said. "We were doing better. We didn't fight like we did back home. All of that was in the past." He tried to sit back, but the cord on the phone pulled taut, stopping him. "We still had our problems, but who doesn't? Things were good between us. I loved her."

I stared at him, didn't speak.

"You're not going to say anything?" He paused, waited. "Your mind is already made up. You think I killed her, and you don't care about what I have to say."

Silent.

"Jesus Christ." His voice was slow, deliberate. "If all you want to do is sit there and stare, then go ahead, but I'm telling you the truth. I didn't kill her."

Nothing.

"You know what your problem is?" Mike leaned closer to the glass. "You're slow to trust and quick to judge. You think you're better than everyone, and that makes you blind. That's what Lilly always said when she talked about you."

I felt a line form between my eyebrows, and I reminded myself to stay calm.

"I used to tell her she was too harsh, but maybe she was right. You've hated me since the day we met, and you've never given me a chance." He held up his hand, as if I might disagree. "I admit, I've given you a few reasons to hate me, but there are two sides to every story, and you never cared about my side." He smiled. "Your sister wasn't like that. She looked for the best in people. She knew things weren't always black and white."

I could tell by the satisfied look on his face that he thought he'd made his point, but I still didn't say anything. Instead, I let the silence between us grow until the look melted away, and his face turned cold.

"I'm wasting my fucking breath with you." He shook his head. "Your sister trusted everyone, and you know it. So instead of sitting there and staring at me like I'm some kind of monster, maybe you should go out and find the person who killed h—" His voice cracked, and he swallowed hard. "That is what you do, isn't it? You're still your father's daughter, right?"

I ignored the comment, and I didn't look away.

He was right about Lilly. She never saw the bad in anyone, including him. She wanted to believe in the goodness of people, and that, as much as anything, was what had killed her. But if I told him he was right, and that I agreed with him, it would only give him hope, and that was something he didn't deserve.

I wanted him to feel the walls closing in around him.

I wanted him to be scared.

"You don't believe me." He waited, frowned. "Of course you don't. I knew you wouldn't. The second I saw you, I knew this would be a waste of time. You'd never believe me, because everything is always my fault with you, and because perfect little Lilly could never do anything wrong in your eyes, isn't that right?" He stopped talking, glanced over at the guard behind him, then back to me. "Well, I've got news for you, Magnolia. Your sister was no fucking angel."

I bit the insides of my cheeks, hard, forcing myself to stay quiet.

"But that doesn't mean I killed her." Mike lifted a hand to his face, rubbed his eyes. "Jesus, Maggie. I was mad, and I lost my temper, but she was alive when I left that night. I didn't kill her. I swear to—"

"Where's my money, Mike?"

He stopped talking. "What?"

I leaned close enough to the glass so he could see my lips, and when I spoke, I kept my voice calm and my words slow so I knew he would understand.

"I said, where's my fucking money?"

Chapter Thirteen

Thomas

That night, Thomas took a pair of needle-nose pliers from his toolbox and carried them into the bathroom. He set the pliers on the edge of the sink, turned the water to hot, and washed the dried blood from around his mouth. His split lip had finally stopped bleeding, but his left eye was swollen and had already begun to bruise.

He studied his reflection, feeling around the inside of his mouth with his tongue. He found the broken tooth on the left side, and gently probed the jagged ridges along the top where it'd cracked.

When his tongue touched the exposed nerve, the pain made him wince.

Thomas took the pliers from the sink, then leaned in close to the mirror and opened his mouth wide. He angled his head in the light as he reached up and secured the pliers around the base of the broken tooth.

Outside, someone knocked at the door.

Thomas paused.

He considered checking to see who it was, but then he heard Lilly's voice through the door, and he turned back to the mirror.

"Thomas? It's Lilly. I wanted to make sure you were okay." She hesitated. "Mike went to the Royale, so if you'd like to talk . . ."

Thomas squeezed the pliers around the broken tooth. Slowly, he began working it from side to side. The pain made his eyes water, and he welcomed it.

"I feel terrible about what I said to you. I think you're a sweet guy, but you barely know me. I'm not the girl for you." She paused. "And you were right about Mike. He was listening to everything, and I knew how he'd react if he heard you."

The tooth gave a little, and Thomas's mouth filled with blood.

"Are you in there?"

Thomas didn't want to hear her, and he squeezed the pliers tighter, trying to block her out. When he did, the tooth cracked and the pliers slipped, digging into his cheek.

The pain was shocking.

Thomas's legs buckled under him, and he grabbed the sides of the sink to keep from falling. All around him the walls wavered in and out of focus, and he closed his eyes, waiting for the pain to pass.

Outside, Lilly asked, "Is everything okay?"

When Thomas opened his eyes, all he saw was blood. It was on his hands, in the sink, on the floor. The pain radiated out from his jaw and into his neck and shoulders, traveling down his spine in jagged waves.

Slowly, he settled into the pain.

Thomas took a deep breath, wiped tears and blood from his face with the back of his hand, and tried to steady himself. When he felt ready, he leaned against the sink and opened his mouth.

His hands shook when he lifted the pliers.

"I guess I'll go," Lilly said. "I won't bother you anymore."

Thomas secured the pliers tight around his tooth, closed his eyes, and pulled hard.

"I hope you understand, and you don't hate me."

He heard a quick series of popping sounds, and he pulled harder.

Finally, the tooth ripped free, covered in blood and skin. He dropped it in the sink and closed his eyes tight. The pain made his stomach twist, and for a brief moment he thought he was going to be sick, but he rode the wave, waiting for the feeling to pass.

Outside, Lilly said, "Goodbye, Thomas. I really am sorry."

Thomas sat on the edge of the bathtub, head down, blood filling his mouth. He leaned over and spit into the sink, then he stood and grabbed a washcloth from the towel rack, and ran it under cold water. He pressed the wet towel against the newly open space in his jaw, then walked out to the living room and stood at the window.

He pushed the curtains aside and looked out at Lilly walking back to her apartment in the dark.

Thomas watched her until she reached the stairs, then let the curtains close.

He went to the freezer and took out several ice cubes and wrapped them in the bloody washcloth. He held the ice against his jaw, then turned the radio on and sat at the small table by the window and closed his eyes.

The radio played one of Chopin's nocturnes.

Thomas lost himself in the pain, and the music, and the blood.

For the next few weeks, Thomas kept to himself.

He spent most of his time sitting at the window, watching Mike and Lilly's apartment, learning their patterns. If he saw them while he was working outside, he would duck out of sight, or he'd take the master key ring from his pocket and slip into one of the vacant apartments and watch them from inside until they were gone.

Always watching.

Sometimes, when he couldn't sleep, Thomas would slip on his hoodie and head down to the shore. The boardwalk at night was always dark and deserted, and he would stand at the far end of the Starlight Pier and stare out into the black. The sound of the sea calmed him, and as he listened, he'd let his mind wander, imagining impossible creatures, massive and indifferent, moving in the nothingness just beyond the light.

On Halloween night, Thomas was leaving his apartment when he heard Lilly laugh. He glanced in the direction of the sound, and when he saw her and Mike coming down the stairs, he stepped back inside and closed his door.

He went to the window and pulled the curtains back.

Lilly was wearing a black flapper dress that came to just below her knees, and Mike had on a dark suit and tie. They were holding hands, and as they approached the El Camino, Lilly bounced around to the passenger side while Mike took the keys from his pocket and unlocked the door. Once inside, they pulled out onto Main Street, heading toward town.

Thomas frowned.

He'd never seen them leaving together, and he'd never heard Lilly laugh when Mike was around. Something about it wasn't right, and the more Thomas thought about it, the more confused he became. The only explanation that made sense was that they were happy, but he refused to believe that.

They couldn't be happy.

Thomas let the curtains close. He walked out of his apartment and down to the main office. He crossed the room to the desk, opened the top drawer, and took out the master key ring. He flipped through the keys until he found the one for unit nine, then he walked out, moving across the empty parking lot and up the stairs to Lilly and Mike's apartment.

He stopped outside, and even though he knew they were gone, he hesitated before sliding the key into the lock and opening the door.

The apartment looked the same as the last time he'd seen it, and he went in, closing the door behind him. There was a stick of incense smoldering in a long wooden burner on the coffee table, and the air had a peppery sweet smell that hung thick and coated the back of his throat, making him gag.

Thomas reached down and pinched the tip of the incense, extinguishing the smoke, then he made his way slowly through the apartment. He stopped in the hall and leaned in close to look at the photograph of Lilly standing with her father and sister in front of those red rocks and blue mountains, but something about it had changed.

The first time he saw the photo, he knew right away which one was Lilly and which one was her sister, but this time he couldn't tell.

They both looked exactly the same.

Thomas went back to the kitchen and took a beer from the refrigerator. He popped the top and drank while he went through their drawers and closets. He stayed awhile in Lilly's underwear drawer, thinking about the pair he had back at his apartment, how he hadn't touched them since the day she . . .

You disgust me.

Thomas frowned, then took another drink before walking out of the bedroom and into the bathroom. He opened the medicine cabinet, touching their toothbrushes, pill bottles, and various creams. He found a pale-yellow plastic shell and clicked it open. The shell was filled with a numbered ring of pills, some blue, some green, some pink.

Half the blue were gone.

Thomas took a drink, then set his beer on the counter. He stepped to the side, opened the lid of the toilet, and popped a week's worth of pills out into the water. He watched as they sank to the bottom, already starting to dissolve, then he unzipped his pants, spit into the water, and urinated. When he finished, he shook off onto the towels hanging beside the shower.

He didn't flush.

He clicked the plastic shell closed and put it back in the cabinet. Then he picked up his beer and walked out of the bathroom.

Thomas moved to the living room, sat on the couch, and drank his beer. Once it was gone, he went back to the kitchen and dropped the empty can in the trash.

When he finally left the apartment, he locked the door behind him.

The next day, Thomas was in the main office when a woman from the rental company called. She told him Lilly and Mike had given notice, that their lease was up, and they would be moving at the end of the month.

Thomas felt nothing.

When she finished talking, Thomas sat down behind the desk and, using his most professional voice, assured her that he'd have the unit cleaned and repainted before the start of the spring season.

"I have no doubt, Thomas."

After they hung up, Thomas leaned back in the chair and picked up the Beaumont Cove snow globe and shook it, watching the snow swirl. He thought about Lilly, wondering if he would be sad when she was gone. He tried to picture the way she'd looked the night they met on the pier, but each time he did, the memory would splinter, and he'd hear her voice echoing sharply in his mind.

You disgust me.

And then he thought of Mike.

A part of him was afraid he'd waited too long, and that his kind and soft nature had failed him. He was sure that Mike thought he'd won, and that it was all over.

Thomas couldn't allow that.

Chapter Fourteen

It was Sunday night, and Thomas watched from the window as Mike left the apartment, got into his El Camino, and pulled out of the parking lot. Once he was gone, Thomas walked down to the main office, went inside, and locked the door behind him. Sunday night was the night Mike threw darts at the Royale, and even though they stayed open until two, he always came home by midnight.

That gave Thomas some time.

He sat behind the desk and turned on the reading light. He took a notepad from one of the drawers and flipped to a clean page. Then he grabbed a pen from the "Welcome to Beaumont Cove" coffee mug next to the reading light and stared at the blank page.

He didn't know where to start.

There was so much he wanted to say, but the words swam in his head, and every time he tried to put them on the page, they rearranged themselves in his mind, and what he'd written sounded thin and meaningless. Each time, he'd tear the page out of the notebook, crumple it, and slide it into his pocket before trying again.

The words wouldn't come, but he kept at it.

By the time he finished, nearly three hours had passed. He looked at the clock. Mike would be home soon. He was cutting it close.

Thomas sat back and read what he'd written:

Lilly,

I understand why you did what you did. At first I thought you said those things to me because Mike was there, but now I know that wasn't the reason. The truth is that you don't share my feelings, and as much as I wish I could make you love me the way I love you, I can't.

These past few weeks have given me time to do some soul-searching, and I believe I'm finally at peace with our situation. I don't blame you for the choice you made, I'm sure it wasn't an easy one. All marriages are complicated, especially loveless marriages, and I wish you nothing but luck with yours.

I want you to know that what we shared meant more to me than just sex. All those days we spent in my bed meant more to me than you'll ever know, and I will always remember how good it felt. No matter what happens, you and I shared something beautiful, and no one can ever take that away.

Goodbye, Lilly.

Thomas

p.s.—I thought I'd return these. You left them at my apartment, and every time I see them, I think of you.

Thomas dropped the pen on the desk and tore the page from the notebook. He folded the paper in half, then reached into his pocket and took out Lilly's black panties and a small gold safety pin. The panties had been well used, and they cracked as he pinned the letter to the fabric. He turned off the reading light, pushed back from the desk, and walked out of the office.

It was almost midnight.

Mike would be home any minute, and Thomas felt a rush of adrenaline as he crossed the parking lot toward Lilly's apartment. When he got to the stairs, he glanced up at the window. There was light leaking through the curtains, and as he made his way up, he could hear music coming from inside.

Once outside her door, Thomas hesitated.

He glanced down at her panties in his hand and ran his thumb over the stiff fabric. He thought about the day he took them from the laundry room and smiled at the memory. His love for Lilly had been so fresh that day, so vibrant, and part of him had thought it would never change.

But he'd been wrong.

Thomas reached down and hung Lilly's panties on the doorknob, looping the straps around twice to secure them in place. Then he turned and walked away. He was halfway down the steps when he saw Mike's El Camino turn into the parking lot.

A rush of panic flooded through him, and he hurried the rest of the way down the steps. He looked across the parking lot toward his apartment, but he didn't think he could make it without Mike seeing him, so he ducked around under the steps to the apartment directly under Mike and Lilly's.

He took the master key ring from his pocket and flipped through the different keys, frantically trying to find the right one.

Mike's headlights passed over the stairs as he pulled into his parking space, and Thomas held his breath until his chest ached. Finally, he found the key, but when he tried to unlock the door, his hands were shaking so much that he couldn't get the key into the lock. He took a deep breath, whispered, "Come on."

He heard Mike's car door open.

Thomas tried the key again, and this time it went in. He turned the knob and stepped into the empty apartment, quickly closing the door behind him. He secured the dead bolt, then he crossed the room to the window and looked out.

He couldn't see much. Most of the window was filled with the bottom half of the stairs leading up to Lilly's apartment, but if he moved to the side, he could just see the corner of his apartment on the other side of the parking lot.

Mike stepped up to the stairs, half stumbling. He had a cigarette in his mouth, and he was shaking a lighter in his hand. He stopped at the foot of the stairs, flicked the lighter several times before it caught, then lit his cigarette. He slipped the lighter into his pocket, then grabbed the railing and started up the stairs.

Thomas stepped away from the window, listening.

He heard Mike's footsteps stop at the top of the stairs, and he held his breath.

Then, all at once, Mike was on the stairs again, his steps heavy and loud.

Thomas went back to the window and watched Mike cross the parking lot, the note, along with Lilly's panties, crumpled in his fist.

When he reached Thomas's apartment, he slammed his fist against the door. The sound was loud, even from across the parking lot. Thomas watched, happy he hadn't tried to make it back to his apartment before Mike had come home.

Mike was shouting, telling him to come outside.

Then, above him, Thomas heard Lilly open the door and step out onto the landing.

"Mike?"

Mike stopped shouting and turned around. He crossed the parking lot toward her, moving fast, his face deep red, his eyes focused.

"What's wrong?" Lilly asked. "What happened?"

Mike didn't say anything, and Thomas watched him through the window as he climbed the stairs. He followed the sound of their footsteps on the floor above as they moved inside the apartment.

The front door slammed, and Mike started screaming at her.

Thomas heard Lilly's voice, muted through the ceiling, as she tried to calm him down. She didn't sound scared, but there was an urgency behind her words as she desperately tried to avoid what she must've known was coming.

The first time Mike hit her, Lilly didn't make a sound. Instead, her voice became harder, more frantic. She begged him to wait, to listen to her, but he didn't.

When the beating stopped, there was only silence.

Thomas strained to listen. At first there was nothing, but then he heard Lilly crying, and when she spoke, there was a tremble behind her words.

"Please," she said. "I don't understa—"

"Liar!"

The rage in Mike's voice was shocking, and it rumbled over Thomas's head like thunder. He heard a slow hissing sound, like something heavy being dragged across the room, and then the unmistakable crash of glass shattering.

Lilly was sobbing, but when Mike began hitting her again, she stopped.

Thomas backed up, moving across the empty room until he felt the wall press against him. Then he slid down to sitting, his legs to his chest, and closed his eyes.

Waiting for it to end.

Chapter Fifteen

When it was over, Thomas stayed on the floor. There were no sounds for a long time. Then, Lilly's apartment door opened, and he heard footsteps moving down the stairs.

He got up and went to the window.

Mike was coming down the steps.

At first Thomas thought Mike might cross the parking lot and go back to banging on his apartment door, trying to flush him out, but he didn't. Instead, he unlocked the door to his El Camino and got in. He sat behind the wheel for a while without moving. Then he started the engine, turned on the headlights, and pulled away.

After Mike had left, Thomas stayed at the window, watching the parking lot, and listening for any noises coming from Lilly's apartment. Once he was sure it was safe, he went to the door, unlocked the dead bolt, and walked outside.

The parking lot was empty, and they were alone.

Thomas stood at the foot of the stairs and looked up at Lilly's window. Then, slowly, he began to climb. When he got to Lilly's door, he lifted his hand to knock, changed his mind, and took the master key ring out of his pocket. He found the one he needed and slid it into the lock.

It turned easily.

Thomas stepped inside, closing the door behind him.

He stood just inside the doorway, scanning the room, listening to the stillness.

At first, nothing looked out of place. Then he noticed the broken glass on the floor in the hallway, and the picture frame lying facedown beside the wall. He stepped forward, hearing the floor creak under his weight, and nudged the broken frame with his foot. He was about to bend down and pick it up when he heard a soft moan coming from the kitchen at the end of the hallway.

Thomas stepped over the broken glass and followed the sound, moving slowly. When he came around the corner, he saw Lilly on the floor. She was leaning against the cabinets, propping herself up with one hand.

Even though he'd thought he knew what to expect, the sight of her shocked him.

Her face was raw and bloody. Her right eye was swollen shut, and when she saw him step into the room, she made a high-pitched whimpering sound in the back of her throat that hung in the air for a long time, unwavering.

Then she began to cry.

Thomas crossed the kitchen toward her, and Lilly followed him with her eyes. When he crouched in front of her and took her hand, she whispered, "It hurts."

"I know."

Lilly's lips were bleeding freely, and heavy black bruises had already begun to form around her eyes. There were thick, finger-sized welts around her throat from where Mike had choked her, and her chest rattled with each strained breath she took.

"I can't breathe," she said. "I need an ambulance."

"I'll call one, but you should lie down," Thomas said. "I'll get a pillow."

As he stood, Lilly held on to his hand, stopping him.

"You were right. I'm sorry."

"Don't worry about that now."

"I was terrible to you," she said, her voice a jumbled wheeze. "I should've listened. I should've gone home, but I thought if I could just—"

She coughed, and a spray of blood landed on the front of her shirt.

Thomas squeezed her hand gently. "Don't talk." He motioned over his shoulder and said, "I'm going to get you a pillow, and then I'll call an ambulance, okay?"

A tear ran down Lilly's cheek, and she nodded.

Thomas let go of her hand and walked back down the hall to the living room. He took a yellow throw pillow, shaped like a smiley face, from the couch. As he started back, he saw Lilly's black panties and his attached note lying on the floor next to the coffee table.

He stared at them for a moment, then went back to Lilly in the kitchen.

Lilly tried to sit up when she saw him. As he knelt in front of her with the pillow, she said, "You're a good friend. I'm sorry I didn't see that."

"Me too."

She started to say something else, but before she could, Thomas leaned forward and, in one quick motion, pressed the pillow hard against her face, slamming her head back and pinning her against the cabinets.

Lilly stiffened and grabbed at his arms and wrists, desperately trying to pull him off. Thomas swung his leg over hers, straddling her, squeezing her hard as he held the pillow against her face, pushing with all of his strength.

"Shhh . . ." he whispered. "It's okay."

Lilly fought longer than he'd expected, but eventually her hands fell away and her legs stopped kicking. He kept the pillow in place while her body twitched under his, and when she was finally still, he eased back and slowly pulled the pillow away.

She looked so peaceful.

Thomas stared at her for a long time. He noticed the silver key on the necklace around her neck, and he reached out, taking it in his hand. He studied the key for a moment, then stood and undid the clasp on the chain, pulling it away.

He slipped the chain and the key into his pocket.

On his way out, Thomas put the pillow back where he'd found it on the couch, then he bent down and picked up the black panties on the floor beside the coffee table. He ripped the note away, crumpled it, and put it in his pocket.

He carried the panties down the hall to the bathroom, opened the lid of the hamper, and dropped them inside. Then he walked back to the living room and left the apartment, closing the door behind him.

When he got to the office, he sat behind the desk and reached for the snow globe and shook it. He took a deep breath and tried to center himself while watching the snow swirl beneath the glass. When he felt ready, he opened the top drawer and ran his finger down the list of emergency numbers, stopping on the one for the sheriff's office. He read it out loud, then repeated it in a whisper as he reached for the phone and dialed.

A woman answered on the third ring. "Sheriff's office."

Thomas cleared his throat. "This is Thomas Bennett at the Orion Lodge on Main Street. I hate to bother you, but I've got a married couple staying in one of the units, and from the sounds of it, they had a pretty bad fight tonight. The husband took off a few minutes ago, but the wife is still inside the apartment, and she's not answering the door. I'm worried he might've hurt her. Can you send someone over?"

The woman kept him on the phone, and Thomas patiently answered her questions while listening to the rapid click of her fingers on the keyboard. She told him a deputy was on the way and to keep an eye out for him.

Thomas thanked her.

After he hung up, Thomas pulled the crumpled note from his pocket and flattened it on the desk. He took a book of matches from the drawer and lit one. Then he lifted the note and touched the match to one corner. The page caught, blackened, and curled. He held the paper until the flames reached his hand, then he turned and dropped it into the empty wastebasket beside the desk.

He watched the note turn to ash.

It was as if it had never existed.

Chapter Sixteen

Later, Thomas stood outside the office and watched two paramedics carry a heavy black body bag out of Lilly's apartment and down the steps toward an ambulance waiting in the parking lot. Sheriff Parks was at the foot of the stairs talking to the medical examiner and taking notes. Occasionally, Lilly's window would flash white above them as the crime scene photographer moved through the apartment taking photos.

Thomas followed everything, lost in the dance.

When he saw Sheriff Parks close his notebook, shake the medical examiner's hand, and then start across the parking lot to where he was standing, Thomas stood up straight and focused his mind on the game. He knew what he needed to do, and who he needed to be, and by the time the sheriff reached him, he was ready.

"Okay, Thomas." Parks opened his notebook and flipped through the pages. "I've got a couple questions, and then I think we'll be done."

"Sure."

Parks stopped on a clean page and looked up at Thomas. "Did you have any contact with the deceased?"

"Lilly?"

Parks nodded, silent.

"I fixed a light switch for her once."

"That's it?"

"Ran into her around here now and then," he said. "And I saw her down on the Boardwalk a couple times."

"How about her husband?"

"Only in passing. We never spoke."

"Did they fight often?"

Thomas nodded.

"Can you elaborate?"

"They fought," he said. "Or at least he would yell at her. Sometimes I'd see her and she'd have bruises on her."

"You never said anything?"

"It wasn't my business," he said. "People have a right to their privacy, but I never thought he'd kill her."

"No one ever does."

Thomas watched as Sheriff Parks wrote in his notebook, then he asked, "Did you find him? The husband? Is he still out there?"

"My deputies picked him up at the Royale about ten minutes ago," Parks said, not looking up from his notebook. "He won't be coming back here, if that's what you're worried about."

"What did he say when they arrested him?"

"That he didn't do it," Parks said. "Standard stuff."

"Do you believe him?"

"I think it's obvious what happened," Parks said. "This wasn't the first time we've had complaints about him. Her husband had a temper, and there was a history here."

Thomas felt a smile build inside of him, and he fought it back. "I can't believe it."

"What part?"

"That he would do this to her," Thomas said. "He didn't seem like the type."

The sheriff stopped writing and stared at him. "I thought you didn't know him."

Thomas heard the suspicious tone in his voice, and he considered his next words carefully. "I didn't, but Lilly seemed so nice. I assumed he would be, too."

Parks made a soft, dismissive sound and went back to writing in his notebook. "That's not how it works."

"No, I guess not." Thomas watched the ambulance pull out of the parking lot, lights off, no hurry. "But I'd like to think you'd be able to tell."

"Tell what?"

"If someone might do this kind of thing," Thomas said. "There should be signs so you know who you're dealing with." He shook his head. "But you're right, that's not how it works."

"Not always."

Thomas glanced at Parks. "You never really know about anyone, do you?"

"I don't know about that," Parks said. "Everyone reveals their true selves eventually. You just have to pay attention."

"You believe that?"

"I have to."

"Why?"

Parks flipped his notebook closed, then clicked his pen and put it back in his breast pocket. "Why what?"

"Why do you have to believe that?"

"Because if I didn't, I couldn't do my job."

That night, after everyone had gone, Thomas sat on the edge of his bed and studied the key he'd taken from Lilly. It was old, silver, and unmarked. There were scratches on the surface, and the chain it was on was aged and dull. He wondered what the key unlocked, and why she'd chosen to wear it around her neck, but after thinking about it for a while, he decided it really didn't matter anymore. Eventually, he stood and slipped the chain over his head, tucking the key under his shirt, close to his heart.

Thomas went into the bathroom and turned on the water in the sink. He washed his face, then took his toothbrush from the medicine cabinet. As he closed the cabinet, he paused for a moment and studied his reflection in the glass. The bruises from his fight with Mike had faded, leaving only the hint of a dirty yellow blush along his cheek and under his eye. His jaw popped every time he opened his mouth, and the spot where his tooth had been still ached, but it was getting better each day.

The realization made him smile.

He thought about Mike sitting alone in jail, and he wondered what he was doing at that exact moment.

Had he gone over his situation in his mind?

Did he know he'd lost?

Thomas felt a sudden jolt of pleasure when he thought about his victory over Mike, but it was tempered by the feeling that it all could have been avoided. The truth, he realized, was that this was all Lilly's fault. If she would've had the strength to do what was right, everything that had happened could've been avoided.

But she didn't.

Lilly waited until it was too late before crawling back to him, telling him she was sorry, and that she made a mistake. She waited until after she'd seen him humiliated and bleeding at her feet before admitting that he'd been right all along.

She'd been a coward, and how could he ever forgive that?

Maybe if they could've started over, gone back to that first night on the Starlight Pier, away from Mike and the memories, then, maybe, they might've had a chance.

But that was impossible.

There were no second chances.

Thomas finished in the bathroom, then walked out and got undressed and climbed into bed, pulling the sheets up around his neck. He listened to the soft wind outside his window and watched the flicker of shadows dance across his ceiling. Then he closed his eyes and told himself, again and again, that everything was exactly the way it should be.

And when he finally fell asleep, he was at peace.

PART TWO

Chapter Seventeen

Magnolia

"How'd it go?" Parks asked. "You were in there for a while. Did you get what you wanted?"

"I got what I expected."

"That doesn't sound good."

We made our way down the hall, past security, and back outside. The dark clouds had moved off toward the horizon, revealing clear sections of evening blue above us. I looked up at the sky as we headed toward the cruiser parked out front and tried not to think about anything.

When we got to the car, I opened the passenger door and slid into the seat as Parks got in behind the wheel. When he pushed the key into the ignition, I glanced over at him and asked, "How many pawnshops are there in this town?"

"Quite a few," he said. "Why?"

"Mike told me Lilly pawned some things after the money ran out," I said. "Things that belonged to our mother, and I want to get them back."

Parks considered this, nodded. "I can give you a couple addresses, places close to where they lived. It'll be a good place to start."

"I can't believe she would've sold any of our mother's things," I said. "But maybe she did. Lilly stopped making sense to me a while ago."

"People change."

It was a throwaway comment, something you say when you don't know what else to say. I knew I shouldn't let it get to me, but it did.

"That's bullshit."

"What?"

"That people change," I said. "It's bullshit."

I saw the muscles in Parks's jaw tighten. He glanced over at me, then back at the road. "You don't think people change?"

"I think saying they do is just a way to justify shitty behavior."

"I guess that's a no?" There was a smile in his voice.

"Lilly used to say it to me every time she went back to him. 'People change, Mags. He's not the same person, Mags. He was going through a tough time, Maggie, and that's why he beat the fuck out of me. That's why I'm eating through a straw, and why I swallow blood every time I smile.'"

I stopped talking, and in the silence, I realized I'd been yelling.

Parks cleared his throat, said, “I’m sorry, I didn’t mean—”

“She told me once that she provoked him.” I laughed, even though it wasn’t funny. “She said it was her fault because she’d pushed him. Can you believe that?”

Parks nodded. “That’s not uncommon in these situations. A lot of times—”

“She was a fucking cliché.” I heard my voice get louder again, but this time I didn’t care. “She became the type of person both of us swore we’d never become, and I can’t understand why she—” My voice cracked, and I paused, took a breath. “People don’t change, Sheriff. They are who they are. It’s the people around us who bring out our true nature. We’re all each other’s angels and demons.”

Parks didn’t say anything, and for a while we drove in silence. I eased back in the seat and stared out the window at the empty fields and the dark clouds waiting low on the horizon. I didn’t want to think anymore, so I focused on the steady rhythm of my breath, and did my best to clear my mind.

Time passed, and then Parks said, “Do you know what you’re looking for?”

“What do you mean?”

“At the pawnshops,” he said. “Do you know what your sister had? Would you recognize the items if you saw them?”

“Of course I would,” I said. “But Mike didn’t know what she kept and what she sold. I’ll have to go from place to place and see what I can find.”

“There might be a better way.”

“What do you suggest?”

"If you had a list of the things she kept, you'd know what was missing. That would make it easier when you search the pawnshops."

"Go through Lilly's things?"

"Seems like the best place to start," he said. "And since you're going to have to go through everything eventually . . ."

He was right, and the fact that it hadn't occurred to me surprised me. "I haven't been looking forward to doing that."

"You could always throw everything away."

"No," I said. "Not all of it."

"You keep what you want, and we'll throw the rest out, or we can donate it," he said. "It'll be a lot of work. Are you up for it?"

"I have to be," I said. "No one else is going to do it."

Parks nodded. "I'll set it up whenever you're ready."

I thought about that, asked, "Are her things in storage?"

"No, everything is still in her apartment."

"Can we get inside?"

"We can," he said. "I even know someone who can help."

Chapter Eighteen

Thomas

Thomas stood over the stove frying two slices of bologna in a cast-iron skillet. He took a plate from the dish drainer and two slices of white bread from an open loaf on the counter and slathered both pieces with mayonnaise while he hummed along to the radio. The classical station was playing Schubert. The music always seemed to put him in a peaceful mood, and when his sandwich was finished, he carried the plate to the small table by the window and sat down. He took a bite and stared out at the empty parking lot, feeling the joy of solitude wrap around him.

It was like sinking into a warm bath.

His day had been a busy one, but also satisfying. He'd finished the last of the repairs on the gutters and had moved on to repainting the top-floor unit in building three. His plan, now that the Orion was empty, was to repaint all the units and have all the repairs finished by the new year. That would give him a few months of uninterrupted quiet before the season started.

The season.

Usually when he thought about the impending summer crowds, his palms would sweat and a dull glow of pain would build behind his eyes, but that didn't happen this time. At that moment, the start of the season seemed like it was a million miles away, nothing more than a distant worry. His plan was to spend the next several months lost in his work, while the crowds of people, and the trouble they brought, were still far away.

Thomas took another bite of his sandwich and wiped the mayonnaise from his mouth with the back of his hand. The bologna was salty and good, and he closed his eyes, savoring the taste as he chewed. He'd been raised by vegans, so it'd taken Thomas a long time to appreciate the taste of meat. At first, he ate it in secret, a small act of rebellion, but eventually, to his surprise, he grew to love it.

Now he wondered how he'd ever lived without it.

He'd finished half the sandwich when a sheriff's cruiser pulled off Main Street and turned into the parking lot. Thomas watched through the window as the car drove past his apartment and parked in front of the main office. He glanced up at the calendar on the wall beside the table. It was still two weeks from the end of the month, too early for the sheriff to stop by and check up on him.

So why is he here?

Thomas got up and leaned closer to the window, angling to see the cruiser at the end of the parking lot. For a while, there was no movement at all, but then the driver's side door opened and Sheriff Parks got out.

Thomas frowned and stepped back from the window. He stuffed the last half of his sandwich into his mouth and chewed as he walked outside.

Parks was standing by the open driver's side door, one arm resting on the roof. From a distance, it looked like he was talking with someone inside the car.

Then the passenger door opened, and she stepped out.

When Thomas saw her, he stopped walking.

All at once his legs felt heavy, and he couldn't move. The wet mass of white bread, mayonnaise, and burnt meat had turned solid in his mouth, and chewing it felt like chewing clay. He looked around, then turned and spit everything into a thin strip of grass beside the sidewalk. Then he stood up straight and wiped his mouth. He took a minute to compose himself before slowly walking toward the office.

Sheriff Parks was approaching the office door, but Thomas wasn't interested in him. He couldn't take his eyes off her, standing beside the car, her arms folded across her chest, one perfect hip leaning against the fender.

He couldn't look away.

"Hey, Tom. There you are." Sheriff Parks smiled and started toward him. "I thought we might've missed you."

"No, I—" Thomas cleared his throat, motioned back over his shoulder. "I was over at my place. It's dinnertime, and I went home to—"

"Well, I'm glad you're here," Sheriff Parks said, cutting him off. "I have a favor to ask of you, and there's someone I'd like you to meet."

Thomas's hands felt slick and wet, and he wiped them on his pants as he moved along the sidewalk toward the cruiser. He kept his eyes down for as long as he could, afraid to look at her, afraid to see that face again.

"Thomas, this is Maggie James," Parks said. "Lilly's sister."

She held out her hand, and Thomas hesitated before taking it. He shook it once, letting go quickly, unable to maintain eye contact. He tried to think of something to say. It seemed easy enough, but when he opened his mouth, there were no words.

"I know." Sheriff Parks laughed. "It's incredible, isn't it?"

Thomas looked up at her, nodded, and this time he managed to say, "It is."

"Listen, Tom. Maggie needs to get into Lilly's apartment. She wants to check for a few items that belonged to her family. Any chance we can trouble you to let us inside?"

Thomas was still staring at her, and he barely heard the question.

"Tom?" Sheriff Parks said. "Is this a bad time?"

"Yeah." Thomas stopped, caught himself. "I mean, no, it's not a bad time, and yeah, I'm fine." He looked from her to Parks and then back to her. "Let me grab the master keys. They're in the office. It'll just be a minute."

"Thanks," Parks said. "We appreciate it."

Thomas moved past him toward the office door. He took his keys from his pocket and fumbled through them with shaking hands. He could feel her eyes on him as he searched, and when he found the right key it took two tries to get it into the lock. Once inside the office, he closed the door behind him and paced the room, his hands on either side of his head, mumbling to himself under his breath.

He needed to calm down.

Thomas reminded himself that this woman was a stranger. She didn't know him, and she didn't know what'd happened between him and Lilly. To her, he was nobody, the maintenance man at her sister's apartment building. That was all. It made sense, but it didn't help, because when he looked at her, Lilly looked back at him.

There was a knock at the door.

"You okay, Tom?"

"I'm good," Thomas said. "Trying to find the key. Be right out."

He moved quickly across the room and opened the desk drawer. The master key ring was on top, but when he picked it up, his hands shook so badly that he almost dropped it. Thomas cursed himself under his breath and leaned forward, his hands on the desk. He knew if he didn't control himself, and he went out there like this, they would get suspicious, and everything would start to fall apart.

Thomas looked up at the door, then down at the open drawer. He moved his left hand to the center of the desk, his thumb hanging over the edge, and slammed the drawer shut, crushing his thumb.

The pain screamed up his arm, cutting through the haze in his brain. Thomas pulled his hand back and put his thumb in his mouth. He shifted his weight from one leg to the other, trying to keep quiet. When the pain began to fade, Thomas bit down hard on his thumb until tears formed in his eyes.

Eventually, he felt his mind clear behind the pain, and his thoughts focused.

Sheriff Parks knocked again, and Thomas took his thumb out of his mouth and stared at his hands.

The shaking had stopped, and his hand was steady.

Thomas smiled, squeezed the keys in his hand, and said, "Found them."

As he moved toward the door, Thomas knew that he'd be okay. They needed him, and he would be happy to help in any way he could. He'd been Lilly's friend, after all, and he did feel terrible about what'd happened to her.

He hoped that maybe, if her sister knew how much he'd cared about Lilly, she would find a small bit of comfort with him. Maybe, if they had a chance to sit and talk, they could share a few of their favorite memories of Lilly. He could tell her how much her sister had missed her, and how often she'd talked about her.

Maybe he could make her smile.

He hoped so.

He'd missed that smile.

Chapter Nineteen

"Here you go." Thomas pushed the door to Lilly's apartment open and stepped to the side. "No one's been in here since—" He caught himself, nodded toward Parks. "Well, since you guys."

"Thanks, Tom." Parks turned to Maggie. "If you'd like to do this alone, we can wait for you out here."

Maggie glanced at him, silent, then stepped forward and crossed the threshold into the apartment.

Thomas watched the way she moved.

It was like seeing a ghost.

"You can stay," she said. "I just want to look around."

"We'll be right here if you need us."

Maggie moved deeper into the apartment. She had her arms folded across her chest as she walked, not touching anything. When she got to the hallway leading back to the kitchen, she stopped and studied the photos hung along the wall.

For a long time no one said anything.

The silence was crushing, and Thomas felt a line of sweat run cold down the middle of his back. He didn't want to be there, but he also didn't want her out of his sight. Seeing her in the apartment again was overwhelming, and his heart felt so full that he thought it might burst open in his chest.

But this wasn't Lilly.

He shifted his weight from one foot to the other, unsure of what to do. Then he noticed Sheriff Parks staring at him, and he tried to smile.

"You okay, Tom?"

Thomas looked over at Maggie, still staring at the photos along the wall, then he stepped closer to Parks and whispered, "They're so much alike."

"Weird, isn't it?" Parks said. "It's a little unsettling."

Thomas nodded. "It's just, I used to see her around here all the time, and—"

Parks reached out and put a heavy hand on Thomas's shoulder. "Try not to think about it. It'll make you crazy."

Thomas laughed, but the sound was wrong. It broke out of him, loud and jittery, and he put a hand to his mouth to stop it, but it was too late.

Maggie looked over at them and frowned.

"Sorry." Thomas cleared his throat and stepped closer. He pointed to the photos. "I like the one of you two with your father. Lilly told me it was the last photo you took together."

The look on Maggie's face softened, and she glanced back at the photo. Then she turned toward him and said, "Lilly had an antique jewelry box." She held her hands out in front of her, a foot apart. "Solid ivory with an ebony base, carved flowers all the way around. Do you know it?"

"Sorry," he said. "I never saw anything like that."

Maggie looked toward the doorway at the end of the hall, pointed. "Bedroom?"

Thomas nodded, and when she started back, he followed her.

"Hey, Tom," Sheriff Parks said. "Why don't you let her—"

Thomas ignored him, kept walking.

He could feel her need radiating from her, and he was powerless against it. The pain, the sadness, the loss she'd experienced, all of it rolled over him like a wave, pulling him toward her. She was going to need someone to be with her, someone who could help her through this time in her life, and he desperately wanted to be that person. He wanted to show her that she could trust him, and that he would be there for her if she needed to talk, or to be held, or even if she just needed . . .

A friend.

Yes, that was where he would start.

Maggie stopped in the doorway and looked around the bedroom. Thomas stood behind her, not wanting to get too close, and looked in over her shoulder. The bed was roughly made, the covers pulled up over two pillows arranged side by side. There was a stuffed turtle between the pillows, and two glass oil candles on the nightstand beside a digital alarm clock flashing a neon-red 12:00.

Maggie stepped into the room.

Thomas shadowed her.

Behind him, he heard Sheriff Parks coming down the hallway, and he felt a flash of anger. He had to stop himself from turning and telling the sheriff to leave, that they didn't need him, and that he could take care of her without his help. But then Maggie stopped at the foot of the bed and spun around to face him.

"Which side of the bed was hers?"

It took Thomas a minute to realize he didn't have an answer.

He didn't know what side of the bed she slept on. How could he? They'd never discussed it, and things had ended between them before he'd ever had the chance to find out firsthand. It wasn't his fault. Still, not knowing something so fundamental about Lilly, something so intimate about the woman he'd loved, upset him on a deep level, and for a minute he couldn't speak.

Then he realized Maggie was watching him, waiting.

"I—" He stumbled over his words. "I don't know."

Maggie turned back to the bed. She hesitated a moment, then walked around to the left side and picked up the stuffed turtle. Thomas saw a thin smile form on her lips and then fade away. She dropped the turtle on the bed and bent down, running her hands under the mattress. When she stood, she was holding a black notebook, and the smile had returned. She opened the notebook, fanned through the pages, and held it up.

"Lilly kept her diary in the same place her entire life," she said. "I told you, Sheriff. People don't change."

A joke?

Thomas's chest tightened.

This was something they shared, just the two of them.

The realization burned inside of him, but only for an instant, because at that moment, all he could focus on was the notebook in Maggie's hand. He'd been through every corner of the apartment, and he thought he knew all her secrets, but he'd missed the diary. He'd never thought to look under the mattress, and now it was too late.

She was going to take it.

The implications slowly dawned on him. He would never get to read what Lilly had written about him, never learn her inner thoughts, or discover the things she thought about while they were together. Those secrets would be lost to him now, forever just outside his reach, even though the diary had been there, waiting for him the entire time.

It was almost too much to bear.

Thomas stepped into the bedroom, his legs moving on their own. As he approached Maggie, he held out his hand.

Maggie frowned and pulled the notebook away.

Thomas lowered his hand, realizing what he was doing, and stepped back. "I'm sorry," he said. "I didn't realize she kept a diary."

The sharp look on Maggie's face softened, and she looked down at the book in her hand. "All her life. I used to ask her why she bothered, and she'd say, 'The unexamined life is—'"

"Not worth living," Thomas said. "Socrates."

Maggie shrugged. "I don't think she knew who said it."

Thomas tried to smile and look casual, but his eyes kept going back to the notebook in Maggie's hand. He wanted the diary desperately, and he fought the urge to reach out and tear it from her hand. It was about him, after all, he knew it. So he should be the one to have it, not her, not anyone else, only him.

"Looks like you have some reading to do back at your hotel," Sheriff Parks said. "I hope it gives you some closure."

Thomas looked at Parks, then back at Maggie. "You're staying in a hotel?"

"Not the one I thought, but yes." She folded her arms, squeezing the notebook against her chest, and scanned the room. "You probably don't know, but Lilly had a necklace. It was a silver chain with a key on it. Have you seen it?"

Thomas felt his face flush, and he shook his head. "I don't think so, but maybe it's around here somewhere."

"It's strange," Maggie said. "I never knew her to take it off."

"I can help you look," Thomas said. "It would be more fun to look with someone to keep you company."

"Thanks," Maggie said. "But I think I'll head over to the hotel. I've had enough fun for one day."

She walked past Thomas and out into the hallway, still cradling the notebook against her chest. Thomas felt his heart speed up, and he followed her, desperate to stop her from leaving.

"Why don't you stay here?"

Maggie turned to face him. Behind her, Sheriff Parks glared at him, a deep line forming between his eyebrows.

"I just mean it would be easier, right?" He cleared his throat. "I could help you go through her things. Two sets of eyes. Maybe together we can find the box you're looking for, or the necklace?"

"Thanks, but I'll stick with the hotel."

Maggie walked away, heading for the door. When she passed Sheriff Parks, he looked up at Thomas and shook his head. Thomas barely noticed. All he could think was that she was leaving, and she was taking Lilly's diary with her.

And there was nothing he could do to stop her.

"I'll give you a ride," Parks said. "The hotel is down at the other end of the boardwalk. Not too far."

"In that case, I think I'll walk. I could use the exercise."

Parks nodded and held the front door for her. He followed her out, and Thomas walked out after them. He locked the apartment door behind him and moved quickly down the steps to keep up. They stopped at the cruiser, and Maggie opened the passenger door. She took her backpack from the seat and set it on the hood, unzipped it, and slid the notebook inside.

Thomas was shaking, and he couldn't do anything but watch as Maggie slipped the backpack over her shoulder. She thanked them both for their help, and then she walked away, heading toward Main Street and the path leading down to the boardwalk.

Sheriff Parks waited until she was out of earshot, then he turned to Thomas. "'Why don't you stay here?'" He shook his head. "Jesus, Tom."

"Maybe I shouldn't have said that."

"Do you think?" Parks laughed, then he walked around the cruiser to the driver's side. "Enjoy your night. I'm sure you'll see us again."

Thomas stayed outside and watched him go, waving as he pulled away. Once the cruiser turned onto Main Street and disappeared, Thomas ran to his apartment, pulled his black hoodie from his closet, and slipped it on as he hurried back outside and headed for the boardwalk.

He hoped she hadn't gone too far.

Chapter Twenty

Magnolia

The walk to my hotel was farther than I'd expected, but I didn't care. The boardwalk was deserted and peaceful, and the only sounds I heard were the heavy rumble of the waves, and the cold rush of the wind coming in off the sea. As I walked past the boarded-up booths, tented rides, and closed stores, I wondered, not for the first time, what Lilly had seen in this strange place, and why she'd chosen to live here.

Part of me thought I understood. Lilly had always been drawn to broken things, people mostly, but it could've been anything that didn't quite fit in. She loved things that seemed lost or forgotten.

Beaumont Cove must've felt like heaven to her.

Sheriff Parks mentioned the town had once been a popular tourist destination, and if I squinted I could almost picture the crowds filling the boardwalk, the families spread out across the beach, the boats drifting on the water. I imagined the Ferris wheel, now a skeletal silhouette against a darkening sky, lit up bright and new, rolling through summer days while the snack booths spun cotton candy and funnel cakes well past dark.

Everywhere I looked, there were ghosts.

I passed by a locked arcade filled with Skee-Ball and coin-operated video games, the walls covered with cheap prizes. Next door, a saltwater taffy shop, and beyond that, a dark window with a silver-white light shaped like a single eye behind the glass. A thick black fabric hung from the ceiling, blocking the view inside. I stepped back and looked up at the storefront, hoping for a clue, but there was only the one glowing eye.

I turned away and looked out toward the sea.

The sun was sinking, and the sky had turned a deep orange along the horizon. There was a line of wooden benches next to the railing, and I crossed the boardwalk, sat down, and watched the seabirds circle and dive along the waterline.

Then I remembered Lilly's notebook.

I slipped my backpack off and set it between my legs. I unzipped the side pocket, took out the notebook, and stared at it for a moment before squeezing it to my chest.

Part of me wasn't sure I was ready to open it.

What if she'd written down everything that'd happened with Mike? I didn't want to read page after page of her making excuses for him. Or worse, what if she didn't say anything about him at all? What if she only wrote down her day-to-day thoughts, trying to pretend everything was normal?

I didn't think I could handle something like that, and I leaned forward to put the notebook back. But before I did, I stopped myself and whispered, "Just the first page."

I opened the notebook.

The pages were filled with sketches.

Most of them were of people, some in groups, some close-ups, and all the faces were unfamiliar. Mixed in alongside the people were detailed sketches of the boardwalk, the Ferris wheel, the arcade. Each one done in pencil.

I didn't understand what I was seeing, and my first thought was that the notebook belonged to someone else. Lilly wasn't an artist. She'd never sketched or painted, never stuck with any of the instruments she tried in school, and she never tried to write poetry or stories or anything artistic. If these drawings were hers, it was something she'd learned how to do after she left home.

The idea of Lilly finding something to be passionate about made me smile, and I flipped through the pages, watching the sketches improve as I turned from the front of the notebook to the back. When I flipped to the last page in the book, my breath caught in my throat, and I stared at the page.

Lilly had done a self-portrait.

I stared at the drawing for a long time, feeling the tears build behind my eyes. After everything that'd happened, I still hadn't cried. I wanted to cry, I needed to cry, but I couldn't do it. When the feeling passed, I closed the notebook and put it back in my backpack and stood up.

I slipped the strap over my shoulder and was about to start walking again when I noticed a man in a black hoodie watching me from the far end of the boardwalk.

I didn't move.

When the man saw me looking, he ducked behind a boarded-up booth with a hand-painted sign above it that read **Cotton Candy** in large pink bubble letters. I turned and looked up the boardwalk toward my hotel, hoping to see someone else, but I was alone.

Slowly, I set my backpack on the bench and unzipped the top. My Taser was inside, and I took it out, keeping my attention focused on the booth where I'd seen the man. I squeezed the grip in my hand, wondering how far I had to go to get to my hotel.

When I was ready, I slipped my backpack over my shoulder and started walking. I was so focused on getting away that I almost didn't notice the neon **Open** sign in one of the shop windows along the boardwalk.

I'd seen the store earlier, with the dark fabric in the windows, and the glowing silver-white eye. I knew the **Open** sign hadn't been on before, but it was now, and as I approached the shop, I turned and looked back at the cotton candy booth.

The man was standing beside the booth, perfectly still, watching me.

A shadow within a shadow.

I felt my heart climb into my throat, then I reached for the door handle and pulled.

I stepped through a split in a black curtain into a dimly lit room with two cushioned chairs and a couch on one side and a glass display counter filled with crystal jewelry, colored candles, and incense on the other. A middle-aged woman sat on a barstool behind the counter. She had a joint in one hand, and she was watching a game show on a small tube television sitting on a shelf beside her.

A thick swell of smoke hung in the air above her head.

I stepped into the room, said, "Are you open?"

The woman turned toward my voice, and she stared at me for what felt like a long time. I was about to ask again, but then she spoke.

"Is the sign on?"

I told her it was.

"Then I'm open."

The woman got up from the stool, shut off the television, and walked around the counter to where I was standing. She had on faded jeans and a long, loose-fitting black shirt that reminded me of a painter's smock, and she wore thick cat-eye glasses.

"I don't get many visitors this late."

"Special circumstances." I looked around the room at the tapestries on the walls and the candles burning in every corner and said, "What exactly do you do here?"

"That depends," she said. "What exactly are you looking for?"

I considered lying, but I changed my mind. "A place to hide."

The woman smiled, showing a gold tooth. "Then this is a place for you to hide." She laughed, put the joint to her lips, and inhaled deeply. She exhaled a huge cloud of sweet smoke into the air, then held the joint out to me.

I thought about refusing, but I didn't.

It'd been a day.

When I tried to hand it back, the woman waved it away. "You keep it, I'm good."

"Thanks." I took another hit, feeling the peaceful space between my brain and my soul bloom and shine. When I looked up at the woman, I smiled. "I think you're the friendliest person I've met in this town."

"Is that right?" Her voice was light and lilted. "Have you met many people here?"

"No." I laughed, took another hit, then motioned to the glass counter. "Crystals, candles, incense, and an all-seeing eye on the window." I paused. "Let me guess, you run a day-care center."

I laughed, but the woman didn't join me.

"Sorry," I said. "It's been a long day."

"When did you arrive?"

"Earlier today."

"And already you're hiding."

I motioned over my shoulder toward the door. "The sheriff told me my hotel was at the end of the boardwalk. I was on my way there, when I saw your sign."

"The Cliff House?"

"You know it?"

"Everyone knows it."

"It's supposed to be nice," I said. "I had another one picked out, but Sheriff Parks moved me. He said I'd be more comfortable, and since all the hotels in town are empty this time of year, I had my pick."

The woman watched me as I spoke, but she didn't speak.

I began to think I was talking too much, so I bit my lips and waited for her to say something. She didn't, and soon the silence moved from awkward to uncomfortable.

"Listen, if you're about to close or something, I can be on my way."

"Not yet," she said. "He's still out there."

"How do you know about him?"

"It's what I do."

"Right," I said. "The eye, the candles. You're a psychic."

"I prefer *observer*," she said. "And you can call me Ava."

"Ava the psychic?" I stopped myself from smiling. "Sorry, Ava the observer."

"Would you like a reading?" she asked. "Since you're here?"

Normally, I would've laughed, declined the offer, and then walked outside to take my chances with the less crazy person stalking me in the dark, but I didn't. Maybe it was the smoke, or maybe it was her kind smile on a very bad day, but whatever it was, I didn't want to leave. If that meant listening to her tell me my future, so be it.

I took another hit off the joint and said, "I don't believe in psychics."

"Most people don't."

I glanced down at what was left of the joint, took one last hit, then looked around for an ashtray. I didn't see one, so I crushed the smoldering tip between my fingers and dropped the roach in my pocket. "I've never had a reading."

"They usually don't hurt."

"How does it work? Do people just come in and you tell them their future?"

"Not exactly," she said. "The universe leads people to me. They're almost always lost or looking for something. I help them figure out what it is they're after, and what the universe wants them to do."

"What the universe wants?" I smiled. "You're starting to lose me."

"The universe led you to me tonight."

"I was being followed and I saw your sign."

"The sign that came on when you needed it to be on?"

I stared at her for a moment, then laughed. "Either I'm really high, or you're fucking with me."

"Maybe both." She smiled. "He's gone, by the way."

"Who?"

"The man following you," she said. "It's safe for you to walk back to your hotel."

"How do you know that?"

"It's what I do."

I stood there, trying to gather my thoughts through the haze, but it was a struggle. The cynical side of me wanted to walk outside and check to see if she was right, but I had a feeling that she was. If I wanted, I could go to my hotel, climb into a hot bath, and then crawl into bed and forget all about this day. But a part of me didn't want to leave.

Something was keeping me there, with her.

Ava must've known I wasn't leaving, because after a pause she put a soft hand on my arm, squeezed gently, and then stepped to the side, motioning for me to follow her.

"Come on back, Magnolia," she said. "Let's see what we can see."

Chapter Twenty-One

Ava led me through a beaded curtain into a dark room. I stopped in the doorway, waiting for my eyes to adjust. Ava struck a match and lit two candles on a small table in the center of the room. There were chairs on either side of the table, and between the candles was a worn deck of tarot cards.

Ava sat down and motioned to the other chair.

I sat across from her.

"I never told you my name," I said.

Ava didn't say anything. Instead, she reached for the cards and shuffled them three times while I looked around the room. The light from the candles was dim, and it didn't reach the walls. Occasionally, I caught glimpses of what looked like carved masks in the darkness, but whenever I tried to make them out, they faded into the shadows.

Ava handed me the cards.

When I took them, she closed her hands over mine, squeezing them along with the cards, and stared at me. Her gaze was steady, but I didn't look away.

Eventually, she let go and leaned back in her chair.

"Cut them, please."

I took the top half of the deck and set it next to the bottom, then I leaned back in the chair and said, "Do you help find lost items?"

"Did you lose something?"

"I didn't lose it," I said. "I just don't know where it is."

Ava reached into the breast pocket of her shirt and took out another joint. She straightened it, then placed it between her lips and took a match from a different pocket. She held the match in the candle flame until it caught, then touched it to the end of the joint and inhaled deeply before handing it to me.

"It's an old ivory jewelry box," I said, taking the joint. "It belonged to my mother. My sister had it, but I think she might've pawned it."

"Did you check the pawnshops?"

"Not yet."

"I'd start there."

I frowned. "Not very psychic."

"No, but it's logical. A lot of times they're the same thing." She smiled at me. "That's a trade secret."

I looked down at the joint in my hand, debated going deeper, then decided that it was too late to turn back and put it to my lips. I held the smoke while Ava flipped cards off the top of the deck and arranged them in a cross pattern between us on the table.

None of it made sense to me, so I asked, “What does all this mean?”

Ava studied the cards, silent, then she held out her hand.

I passed the joint to her, then shifted in my seat to get a better look at the images on the cards. I didn’t know what any of them meant, but one stood out to me. On it, a skeleton in black armor rode a white horse through a battlefield littered with bodies. At the bottom of the card, one word:

Death.

I pointed to the card and said, “That doesn’t seem good.”

“I’m not sure yet,” Ava said. “But it doesn’t mean what you think.”

“It doesn’t mean I’m going to die?”

“It represents change following an event or a loss,” she said. “It’s an ending, but also a new beginning. The placement of the card is your foundation. Something happened, and now the person you used to be is gone.”

I didn’t say anything.

Ava stayed focused on the cards, touching them one by one, not looking up. “You lost someone close to you.” She paused. “No, not just close, someone who was a part of you on a fundamental level.” She looked up at me. “A sibling?”

I opened my mouth, stunned, but no words came out.

Ava looked back at the cards. “There was bad blood between you,” she said. “But also a deep and unbreakable love.”

“We were twins.”

"You held each other up," she said. "After a great loss. A parent?"

I tried to swallow, but my mouth was dry, so I looked away. I didn't want to be there anymore, but something wouldn't let me get up and walk out. So instead, I focused on the shadowed faces of the masks hanging on the walls just beyond the candlelight.

"You betrayed her."

"Excuse me?"

Ava looked up from the cards. "You turned your back on her when she needed you," she said. "There was a fight."

"I betrayed her?" I shook my head. "You don't know what you're talking about."

"Are you sure?"

"After what I did for her? What I sacrificed?" I bit the insides of my cheeks hard, looked away. "She tossed me aside, and I had every right to be angry."

Ava watched me as I spoke, silent.

I took a deep breath, forcing myself to calm down. "I'm sorry."

She held the joint out to me, but I waved it off.

Ava put it to her lips, and I watched the tip glow red. Then she said, "Your sister couldn't toss you aside even if she wanted to. Neither of you could. You were bonded."

I laughed, softly. "The cards told you that?"

"The cards don't tell me anything," she said. "They're guideposts. They show me where to look to find the answers, that's all."

"I'm not convinced," I said. "What do they say is coming up? Do you have any good news for me?"

"Of course," she said. "Although this one is troubling."

Ava tapped her finger on one of the cards. I leaned closer and saw the figure of a man covered in blood, lying facedown on the ground with a forest of swords sticking out of his body.

"What is it?" I asked.

"The ten of swords." Ava studied the cards, then shook her head. "I need some time with these. Can you come back another day?"

"I don't plan on being in town for long," I said. "It'll take a day or two to get things in order, and I still have to call pawnshops and try to find my mother's jewelry box, but then I'm leaving."

"Talk to Clay Jenkins." Ava didn't look up. "He has an office in the Atrium Building. It's by your hotel. He'll be there tomorrow, but never before noon."

"Clay Jenkins?"

"He's a private investigator," Ava said. "He used to be the sheriff in his younger days, and he knows every inch of this town. If anyone can help you find the jewelry box, he can. Make sure you tell him I sent you."

"Thanks, but I'm sick of cops. I think I'll just call around and see if I can track it down on my own. I did some PI work myself back home."

"Yes, I know," Ava said. "Except Beaumont Cove isn't Manitou Springs."

"How do you—"

"Go see Clay. You'll like him, and he'll like you."

"I doubt it," I said. "I'm not the easiest person to get along with."

"You'll get along with him."

"How do you know that?"

Ava looked up from the cards and leaned back in her chair. "Because Clay Jenkins is a man with a fork in a world of soup," she said. "Just like you."

I didn't want to smile, but I couldn't help it. "Thanks, but I think I'll see how I do on my own first."

"Suit yourself."

Ava turned back to the cards, and I pushed away from the table and stood up. I thanked her for letting me hide for a while, and she mumbled something under her breath without looking up.

As I made my way toward the beaded curtain leading to the front of the shop, I stopped and turned back. "Do you really believe all this psychic stuff?"

"Does it matter what I believe?"

"You're dodging my question."

Ava looked up, her eyes narrow. "The night your father was killed, you had a dream where he told you that you and your sister would be okay if you stuck together. He told you he would watch over you both. Do you remember?"

"How the hell do you—"

"'There are more things in heaven and earth.'" She looked back at the cards. "Good night, Magnolia. Pull the door closed when you leave."

I hesitated, then walked out.

When I stepped outside, the **Open** sign was off, and the cool night air cut through the haze in my mind. I pulled the door closed, hearing the lock catch, then stood for a moment, scanning the boardwalk.

When I was sure I was alone, I began walking.

My mind was still running slow from the smoke, and the more I thought about what Ava had said, the less I understood. I told myself I'd think about it tomorrow.

I walked the rest of the way, wondering what the hell kind of town I'd landed in.

Chapter Twenty-Two

Thomas

Thomas watched her disappear into the witch's shop, and for a long time he didn't know what to do. He considered following her inside but rejected the idea. She'd already seen him following her, and even though he didn't think she'd recognized him, if he went into the shop after her, she would know.

The thought of being exposed and having to see the look on her face when he explained why he was there made his stomach cramp. He could tell her the truth, that he was following her because he was curious. But he knew that no matter how well he explained himself and the situation, she wouldn't understand.

Women never understood.

So instead, he listening to the rumble of the sea behind him, and he waited.

After a few minutes, the **Open** sign above the door went dark.

It took Thomas a minute to register what had happened, but even then he didn't understand. She was still inside. He'd never seen her come out. Had he missed her? Was it possible she'd left through a back door?

Thomas stepped out from behind the booth and slowly made his way toward the witch's shop. He had to know where she had gone, but his legs felt weaker with each step, and he was having a hard time catching his breath.

What if she was still inside?

What if she came out of the shop and saw him?

Thomas felt his heart climb into his throat, and he stopped and looked around.

If she came out now, he'd have no place to hide. She would see him. She would know he'd been following her, and no matter what happened from then on, she would be lost to him forever.

It was time to leave.

He hated the idea, but he had no choice.

As he walked back up the boardwalk, he reminded himself that this was a new beginning. No, she wasn't Lilly, and he would need to be patient with her, but the universe had given them a second chance, and he couldn't rush it. If he scared her away, she would close off to him, and it would end before it began.

He had to make her feel comfortable, gain her trust.

Once she trusted him, he might decide to tell her the story of how he had followed her along the boardwalk the night they met, and how she'd almost caught him. He imagined her surprise when she found out it had been him admiring her from a distance, the coy smile, the shy, flattered blush on her cheeks.

It would make a good story, romantic and funny.

One they could tell at parties.

This is how we met.

By the time Thomas got back to the Orion, he thought he knew what he needed to do. He went to the office and took the master key ring from the desk, then climbed the stairs to Lilly's apartment and went inside. He'd spent so much time in the apartment since the night Mike was arrested that he thought he knew it as well as his own, but that obviously wasn't true. It had taken five minutes for Maggie to find Lilly's diary, and if he'd missed that, he could've missed something else.

If he found the ivory box for Maggie, she'd be grateful.

And then, maybe, she would start to trust him.

Thomas flipped the overhead light and closed the door behind him. He'd been through the apartment, checking the drawers, closets, and shelves, and he didn't remember seeing an ivory box. Of course, he hadn't been looking for one, so he would go through everything again. If the box was somewhere in the apartment, he would find it.

Thomas started in the bedroom.

This had been his favorite room, and he'd spent the first couple of nights after Mike was arrested going through Lilly's closets and drawers, taking out different outfits and laying them across the bed, one at a time. He would imagine her there with him, wearing the clothes he chose for her. Then, slowly, he would reach down and unzip his pants before lifting the hem of a dress, or pulling the shoulder of a blouse down to reveal the delicate fabric of the underwear lying beneath.

This didn't last long, and he would wake up the next morning in Lilly's bed, surrounded by her clothes, with his pants down around his thighs. Then he would get up, clean himself in the bathroom, and put everything back the way it'd been, careful to not leave a mess before walking out into the morning light.

Another night, Thomas just sat on the couch and imagined that he shared the apartment with Lilly. He'd convince himself that she was working late, and then he'd take a beer from the refrigerator, kick off his shoes, and sit back with his feet on the coffee table, waiting for her to come home to him.

And the hours passed.

It didn't take long for Thomas to grow bored with the apartment. He'd been through everything inside, seen all there was to see, and no matter how hard he tried to lose himself in the fantasy of his life with Lilly, there was always something there to remind him of Mike, and it would break the spell.

Eventually, Thomas stopped going altogether.

It didn't bother him too much.. He'd seen all there was to see in the apartment, which was why he was surprised when he opened a cabinet in the bathroom and found, sitting underneath a stack of old magazines, an intricately carved ivory box with a polished, dark wooden base.

Thomas inhaled one sharp breath, then reached in and moved the magazines. He took the box from the cabinet and held it in front of him, turning it over in his hands and running his fingers along the surface and over the keyhole on the front.

Then he remembered Lilly's key.

Thomas reached up and grabbed the chain around his neck and pulled the key out from under his shirt. He slipped the chain over his head and tried the key in the lock.

It went in easily, but it wouldn't turn.

Thomas frowned.

He pulled the key out of the lock and stared at it for a moment before putting the chain back over his head and tucking the key under his shirt. After the pain of losing Lilly's diary, he had to know what was inside the box, and why Maggie was so intent on finding it. For a second, he considered taking it to his workbench in the shed and breaking the lock open, but he knew if he did that, he would lose any chance of proving to Maggie that he was on her side, and that she could trust him.

That was the most important thing of all.

But the temptation was strong.

In the end, Thomas took the box back to the bathroom and replaced it in the cabinet, burying it under the stack of magazines just like he'd found it.

When the time was right, he'd discover it all over again.

Just for her.

Chapter Twenty-Three

Magnolia

I awoke to sunlight, and the soft tap of someone knocking at my door. The bed was huge and soft, and I didn't want to get up. Part of me hoped whoever was knocking would just go away, but they didn't, and eventually I threw back the covers, slipped into the complimentary Cliff House robe, and stumbled to the door.

The girl standing in the hallway looked no older than sixteen. She took a step back when she saw me, and immediately started apologizing. She was wearing a hotel uniform, and her name tag said Natalie. She had a manila envelope in her hand with my name written in black Sharpie on the front. I stared at the envelope ahd waited for her to hand it to me. When she didn't, I pointed to it and said, "Is that for me?"

Natalie looked down at the envelope in her hand, as if seeing it for the first time, and quickly held it out to me. "Yes, it came from the sheriff's department. We wouldn't have bothered you this early, but they said to bring it to your room and make sure you got it first thing this morning. We figured it was important, so we—"

"What time is it?"

"Eight thirty," she said. "There's only a few guests, but we still have coffee in the lobby, or you can order room service. The restaurant is—"

"Thank you," I cut her off, then held up the envelope. "For bringing this."

"No trouble. If you need anything, just—"

I closed the door and walked back to the bed. I picked up the phone and ordered a pot of coffee from room service, then I opened the envelope. There was a single sheet of paper inside with a list of phone numbers. Next to each number was the name of a pawnshop.

It was too early for that, so I dropped the envelope on the nightstand next to the phone and lay back on the bed, staring up at the ceiling. Coffee came first, and then I'd start calling pawnshops. With any luck, I'd find everything I wanted early and be out of this town in a day or two. It sounded like a good plan at first, but when I thought about returning to Manitou, I felt a cold ache twist in the pit of my stomach.

I sat up, pushing all thoughts of home away, then I crossed the room to the glass doors leading out onto the balcony. I pulled the curtains back, opened the doors, and stepped out into the crisp morning air. The sky over the sea was clear and blue, and the sunlight reflected silver off the water. The Ferris wheel looked small from the balcony, and I leaned against the railing, watching the scatter of people move up and down along the boardwalk.

I stayed on the balcony until my coffee arrived. Then I went inside, poured myself a cup, and grabbed the list of numbers off the nightstand.

I started at the top.

It took less than half an hour to call them all. I told them who I was, and explained the situation. Then I described every detail of the ivory box, but no one had seen it or had anything like it.

After I dialed the last number on the list, I finished my coffee, then I went into the bathroom to shower. I did my best thinking in the shower, and I hoped something would come to me, but it didn't. It seemed like my only option was to go back to Lilly's and search her things, and hope I got lucky. But if what Mike had told me was true, I didn't think I'd find anything.

I needed help.

My thoughts kept returning to my conversation with Ava from the night before. Large parts of that conversation were cloudy, but I remembered her mentioning a friend, and that I would need help from someone who knew the town. I didn't like the idea of working with a private investigator, but I also wasn't about to leave town without doing everything I could to find my mother's things.

I had to think about it.

By the time I got out of the shower, I'd made my decision.

I got directions to the Atrium Building from a red-faced, round man working at the front desk of the hotel. The building was three blocks away, and when I got there, I searched the directory in the lobby, stopping on the name *CJ Investigations*.

Second floor, suite 217.

I took the stairs and walked along the hallway until I came to a door with **CLAY JENKINS INVESTIGATIONS** stenciled on the frosted-glass window.

I tried the handle.

It was locked, so I knocked on the glass and waited.

When no one answered, I knocked again, louder. This time I heard footsteps from inside, and when the door swung open, a man in his late fifties wearing a pink-and-white-striped bathrobe glared down at me. His thick gray hair stood off his head in all directions, and his face was covered in a thin patchwork of stubble.

For a moment, neither of us spoke. Then he said, "What?"

"My name's Maggie James." I hesitated. "A woman on the boardwalk named Ava recommended you. She said to tell you she sent me."

"Did she also tell you to come this damn early?"

"Excuse me?"

"What the hell time is it?"

I didn't have a watch, so I just looked at him and shrugged.

Clay frowned. “That explains it,” he said. “It’s too damn early, that’s what time it is. I don’t open until noon.”

“Should I come back?”

“No, goddamn it. I’m up, might as well stay up.” He backed away from the door, motioning for me to follow. “Find a place to sit, and I’ll be with you in a minute. Just let me throw some clothes on and start the coffee.”

Slowly, I stepped into the office. There was a couch covered with pillows and a thin green blanket against one wall. Next to it, a cluttered desk, two plastic chairs, and a large french window shielded by dusty venetian blinds.

Clay disappeared into a second room, closing the door behind him.

“Do you live here?” I asked.

“Does it matter?”

It didn’t matter, at least not to me, but I didn’t say anything. Instead, I sat in one of the plastic chairs, crossed my legs, and waited.

When Clay came out, he was wearing gray pants and a faded Hawaiian shirt with electric-blue palm trees and half-naked hula girls dancing in front of an orange sunset. He walked around behind his desk, took a stack of papers from his chair, and looked for someplace to put them. Eventually, he set them on top of more papers sitting on his desk.

Then he sat down and stared at me. “So, the witch sent you?”

I frowned. “If you’re talking about Ava the psychic, then yeah.”

"First time you met her?"

"It was."

"And how was that for you?"

"A little creepy."

Clay almost smiled. "Let me guess, she got you high and told you things about your life that no one else knows."

I sat there, letting his words sink in, then said, "Are you saying she scammed me?"

"A carnival fortune-teller who caters to short-stay tourists?" He chuckled to himself. "No, not a chance."

"But the things she knew," I said. "No one knows about that stuff but me and . . ."

The silence hung in the air.

"You and?"

"Just me," I said. "She knew things that only I know."

"You were going to say you and Lilly."

"How do you know about—"

"Everyone on the boardwalk knew Lilly," he said. "She worked at the Mercury Café down by the arcade. We all eat there, and she was always around. At least until her husband made her quit."

"You knew her?"

"Of course I did," he said. "She was one of us."

"And Ava knew her."

"Lilly was one of her regulars," he said. "So yes, it's safe to say she's heard all about you and what happened between the two of you."

I felt a sudden flash of anger, and I turned away, shaking my head.

When I looked back, Clay was smiling.

"Ava can be infuriating," he said. "Believe me, I know. I was married to the woman for almost twenty years. Better to let it go and look at it for what it is, a good story." He stopped. "She didn't charge you, did she?"

"No."

"Okay." He nodded. "Because that would be different."

"Still," I said. "Who does that kind of thing?"

"What's important to ask is did she point you in the right direction?" He sat back in his chair, held his arms out to his sides. "She led you to me, so I'd say she did."

"We'll see about that."

"I suppose we will," Clay said, grinning. "Now let's talk about why you're here."

Chapter Twenty-Four

I told Clay about the ivory box and all the other things I remembered Lilly taking when she left home. He listened as I listed the pawnshops I'd called that morning, and when I finished he reached across his desk and took a pencil from a coffee mug and flipped over what looked like a flyer for a Chinese restaurant and began to write.

When he finished, he dropped the pencil and looked up at me.

"The pawnshops were a good place to start," he said. "Was the box real ivory? If it was, and if it's as old as you say, it could be worth real money."

"My great-grandfather bought it for my great-grandmother before he came home from the war. It's real ivory. Probably illegal, definitely valuable."

Clay nodded. "There are a couple different avenues I can explore," he said. "I'll talk to some people who don't always work in the light. Knowing your brother-in-law and his friends, we might have more luck checking the black market."

"Can I help?"

"Do you have a list of everything that's missing?"

"I still need to go through Lilly's things," I said. "But I've been avoiding going back to her apartment."

"I'd need a list."

"I know."

He hesitated. "Would you like to put this off until you feel more comfortable?"

There was a note of condescension in his voice, and even though it was directed at me, it still made me smile. It sounded like something I'd say if I were on that side of the desk, and it made me think about what Ava had said about us getting along.

"I can go over and look," I said. "I'll get you a list by tomorrow."

"Oh, good," he said. "In the meantime, I'll call around and put together my own list of people who might know something."

Clay went back to writing on the flyer, and I waited, silent. After a while, he looked up at me and asked, "Are you planning on staying?"

"No." I scoffed. "Once this is taken care of, I'm on the first bus out of town."

"I meant here, in my office."

This time, I laughed out loud. Then I stood up and started for the door. Before I walked out, I turned and looked back.

"If I was a private investigator, and my ex was a carnival fortune-teller who catered to tourists, it would make sense to work together," I said. "Seems to me that she could send a lot of people your way, if there was something in it for her."

Clay stared at me for what felt like a long time, and I could see the smile building behind his eyes. Then it was gone, and when he spoke, his voice was even and soft.

"We were both sorry about what happened to your sister," he said. "She was a wonderful person. If we can help you, we will help you."

I felt my throat tighten, and it took a minute before I could speak. When I could, I thanked him, then left his office, walked back down the stairs, through the front doors, and out into the cold November sun.

I wasn't in a hurry to get to Lilly's apartment, so I took my time as I walked along the boardwalk. Several of the shops were open for business, and occasionally I'd stop and look in the windows. There were gift shops, a custom jeweler, a glassblower, and a sweets shop that made and sold their own saltwater taffy.

All of them empty.

I passed a few people along the way. None of them looked at me, and they all moved quickly, as if they had someplace to be. It was easy to tell they were locals, and each time I passed one of the empty shops, I wondered how much business a gift shop or a glassblower would do when all the tourists were gone.

I was trying to imagine what Beaumont Cove must've been like during its heyday when I noticed the cotton candy booth up ahead, and I realized I was at the spot where I'd seen the man following me the night before.

I turned and looked at the shops to my left.

The white eye behind the glass.

Part of me wanted to go in. I even took a step toward the door before stopping myself. I had things I needed to take care of, and confronting Ava for lying to me about Lilly was not high on my list. Also, I wasn't that angry about it.

I just didn't like being lied to.

And maybe Clay was right. Ava did recommend him to me, and he seemed to know the town. He also wanted to help. I had no hope of getting my money back, but I refused to leave town without my mother's things.

All I had to do was find them.

I reached the pier at the end of the boardwalk and made my way up the path leading to the Orion Motor Lodge. I crossed the street and cut through the grass to the main office building. The door was locked, so I knocked and waited.

No answer.

I leaned closer to the glass, shielding the glare with my hands. It looked dark inside, and I didn't see any movement, but

I knocked again just to be sure. This time when no one answered, I stepped back from the door and looked around, frowning.

The parking lot was empty, and the buildings all looked deserted.

I cursed myself under my breath for not calling to see if anyone would be here to let me into the apartment. It'd been a long walk, and it looked like it'd been for nothing.

All I could do was wait and hope someone showed up.

Luckily, I didn't have to wait long.

Thomas, the man Sheriff Parks had introduced me to the day before, came around the corner carrying four paint cans, two in each hand. He had a folded blue tarp under one arm and a roller brush pinned under the other.

He didn't see me right away, so I held up one hand and said, "Hello, again."

When Thomas saw me, he jumped back, startled. He dropped the brush and two of the cans. One of the paint can lids came off when it hit the sidewalk, and an eggshell wave spread over the cement and into the grass.

I moved to help, but Thomas stopped me. He tried to pick everything up, but his entire body seemed like it was shaking, making it tougher than it needed to be.

I watched him struggle for a moment, then stepped closer. "Can I help?"

"No, I got it."

"I didn't mean to scare you."

"You didn't." He dropped the brush again, and this time it landed in the paint. Thomas reached down to pick it up, pinning it again under his arm and coating his hand and shirt with paint. "Okay, maybe a little."

"Let me take something." This time I insisted. "Hand me those cans."

"You'll get paint on you."

"I don't care."

Thomas looked up at me, and for a second I thought I saw confusion behind his eyes. He glanced down at the cans in his hand, seemed to consider his next move, then handed them to me and said, "Thank you."

"Least I could do," I said. "Where are you taking them?"

He pointed to the door behind me. "I'm repainting all the units this off-season, including the office."

I waited until he'd picked everything up, then I stood back as he unlocked the office door and went inside. I followed, setting the cans on the floor by the door.

"I was wondering if you could let me into the apartment. I want to take another look around. Didn't have much luck with the pawnshops."

"Yeah, sure," Thomas said. He looked at the paint on his hands, then walked over to a counter with a coffeepot and a small sink. There was a roll of paper towels hung on the wall, and he pulled several off and wiped his hands. "Let me get cleaned up a little, and I'll go over with you."

"Thanks."

I waited as he struggled with wiping the paint from his hands. Eventually, he gave up and gathered the used paper towels and carried them to the wastebasket. Then he moved to the desk, opened the top drawer, and took out a ring of keys.

"You know, I'm not doing anything right now," he said. "I'd be happy to help you search. There's a lot of stuff to go through over there. It seems like a two-man job."

"I thought you were painting."

"I can do that anytime."

"I don't know," I said. "I don't want to be any trouble."

"No trouble. I want to help," he said. "Lilly was always kind to me. If I can do anything to make any of this easier for you, I want to."

I didn't like the idea of being alone in Lilly's apartment with him. He wasn't a big man, and he didn't seem like a threat, but there was something about him that didn't sit right. I couldn't put my finger on it.

"Did I make you uncomfortable?" he asked.

"No," I lied. "Not at all. It's just that . . ."

I let my words trail off while I tried to think of a way to say no without having to say no, but nothing came to me. Also, he was right. It was a big job, and it would be easier with two people.

"Okay," I said. "I'd appreciate the help."

"Great," Thomas said, smiling. "I won't get in your way. I promise."

Thomas spun the key ring on his finger, then moved quickly, almost bouncing, toward the door. I followed behind him, trying to ignore the cold feeling settling in the center of my chest, and hoping I hadn't just made a mistake.

Chapter Twenty-Five

I followed Thomas up the stairs to Lilly's apartment and waited while he slipped the key into the lock and pushed the door open. He stood to the side and held out his arm, guiding me through the doorway.

"After you."

I took a deep breath, steadying myself, then I stepped over the threshold and looked around at the living room. "I don't know where to start."

"Pick a room," Thomas said. "If you want to start in here or the bedroom, I can check the bathroom or the kitchen."

"I'll start in the bedroom." I looked over at Thomas. He seemed so happy to help that I wondered if I'd misjudged him. Lilly used to tell me that there were still good people in the world, and I tried to keep that in mind. "Thanks for helping. I'm glad you're here."

Thomas's face flushed and he looked away.

"I didn't mean to embarrass you," I said.

"You didn't." He briefly made eye contact, breaking it just as quickly and motioning toward the hallway. "I'll start in the bathroom."

I watched him turn the corner, then I crossed the room to the bookshelves against the wall. "Did you know my sister?"

"Not really," he said from the bathroom. "I saw her around a few times, and I fixed a light switch for her once. She told me about you."

"Did she?"

"Just small talk. She told me your dad was the only person who could tell you apart."

"She liked to think that."

"It wasn't true?"

"To strangers, sure," I said. "But once you got to know us, it was easy to tell who was who. There were differences."

"Your voice is deeper," Thomas said. "And your smile is different."

I glanced in the direction of his voice. "My smile?"

Thomas stuck his head around the corner and pointed to the photos along the wall. "The photo of you two with your father. You can see the difference."

I nodded and turned back to the shelves, thinking of the photo.

I remembered the day it was taken. It was the last time the three of us were together, a few weeks before my dad was killed, and before Lilly began seeing Mike. We'd met for lunch at a small place in Manitou, and then we hiked through the

Garden of the Gods, laughing and talking, believing things would never change.

"Did you know Mike?" I asked. "Lilly's husband?"

Thomas was quiet for a moment, then said, "No, I never talked to him."

"I heard he made her quit working," I said. "Didn't she have a waitress job at some diner on the boardwalk?"

"I don't know. When I met her, she stayed home most days." He paused. "Maybe it says something in her diary. Did you get a chance to read any of it?"

"Turns out it wasn't a diary," I said. "It was a sketch pad."

"Lilly was an artist?"

"Apparently she was," I laughed. "That was something new."

"There wasn't anything in the notebook?" he asked. "She didn't write anything about her life here?"

"Not a thing."

Thomas was quiet.

"It's too bad in a way," I said. "I don't know what happened with Mike, but I would've liked to know what things were like for her here."

"He wasn't good to her." Thomas hesitated. "I'm sorry, I don't know if you want to hear any of this."

"What do you know?"

"I'd see her from time to time," he said. "Sometimes she'd have bruises."

I felt a familiar ache settle in my chest, and I kept quiet.

"I asked her about it once," he said. "She told me she bruised easily, so maybe—"

"That's bullshit." There was an edge to my voice, but I didn't care. "She used to say the same thing to me when she'd come home with . . ."

I stopped, bit down hard.

Deep breaths.

Thomas came around the corner. "I'm sorry. I shouldn't have said anything."

"It's not your fault," I said. "Have you found anything?"

"No, I—"

"You're lucky you didn't know him," I said, not ready to let it go. "Did you know the first time I met him, he grabbed my ass and tried to kiss me? He'd only been dating Lilly for a few weeks."

"Maybe he thought you were her."

"No, he was thinking threesome," I said. "It's a twins thing. There's always some walking cliché out there trying to double up."

"Did you tell her?"

"Of course I told her," I said. "He wasn't the first to have the idea, not by a long shot, but he was the first she let stick around."

"Why would she do that?"

"If I knew, we wouldn't be here now."

For a while, we searched in silence. I did my best to push the thoughts of Mike and Lilly out of my head, but it was tough to do surrounded by all their things. Instead, I stayed focused on the job. I went through the rest of the living room, searching the shelves, the drawers, under the couches, but I didn't find anything.

"I'm going to try the kitchen," I said. "There's nothing in the living room."

"Okay," Thomas said. "I think I'll—"

I waited for him to go on. When he didn't, I said, "Find something?"

"I don't know." Thomas came out of the bathroom holding the ivory box in his hands. "Is this what you're looking for?"

"You found it." I ran to him and took the box, turning it over, studying all the sides, the top and bottom. "Where was it?"

"In the bathroom cabinet, buried under some magazines."

"Thank you, thank you."

I wrapped my free arm around his shoulder, half patting, half hugging him. Thomas stiffened under my arm. He made a soft sound in the back of his throat, and when he hugged me back, I felt him tremble.

I pulled away and looked down at the box, running my finger over the keyhole. "You didn't find a silver key back there by any chance, did you?"

"No, I—" His voice cracked, and he cleared his throat. "This was all I saw."

"Hey, it's a start," I said. "Thank you again."

Thomas leaned in, and I moved back fast. I started to ask him what the hell he thought he was doing, but all he did was reach out and touch the lid of the box and say, "It looks hand carved."

I felt a sudden mixture of relief and embarrassment. I covered both with a smile, but I still kept some space between us.

"It is hand carved," I said. "I don't know who did it, but this box has been in my family for at least a hundred years."

"I'm glad I found it."

Thomas stared at me, and there was a look in his eyes that I'd never seen before.

"So what are you going to do now?" he asked. "Are you hungry? We can grab lunch on the boardwalk, then come back and keep looking. Maybe we can find the key."

"Thanks, but there's someone I need to see."

"Who?"

I frowned. "Someone."

I thought the tone in my voice was obvious, but Thomas didn't catch it. He barely seemed to notice that I'd spoken at all. Instead, he nodded along, staring at my lips as I spoke, and I watched the light behind his eyes turn dark.

"I should get going," I said. "Next time?"

"It's a date," he said.

I paused. "That's not what I meant."

Thomas jerked back and stood up straight, as if he'd been struck. "Of course," he said. "I'm sorry, I didn't mean—"

"It's fine."

"I really wasn't implying—"

"It's okay."

Thomas nodded, and I noticed the odd look I'd seen in his eyes was gone.

We left the apartment, locking the door behind us, and walked down the steps to the parking lot. I thanked Thomas again for his help, but when I turned away and started toward the boardwalk, he called after me.

"I'm sorry if I upset you," he said. "I like talking to you, that's all."

I told him again that it was okay, then I said goodbye and walked away.

As I crossed the street to the path leading down to the boardwalk, I turned and glanced back at the parking lot. Thomas was still there, standing in the same spot. He had his hands to his sides, and he was watching me.

I waved, but he didn't wave back.

Chapter Twenty-Six

On my way back to my hotel, I stopped at the Atrium Building and went up the stairs to Clay's office. This time the door was unlocked, and when I went inside, the blankets and pillows were off the couch and Clay was sitting behind his desk, writing on a yellow legal pad. He watched me over the top of his reading glasses as I came inside, and when he saw the ivory box in my hand, he eased back in his chair, took off his glasses, and tossed them on the desk in front of him.

"Looks like you didn't need me after all."

"Blind luck," I said. "I hope you didn't spend too much time on it."

"Not a lot." He ripped the page out of the notepad and stood up. "I was about to drive up north to see a friend of your brother-in-law's. He used to hang around with him and your sister. If they were selling your family's things, there's a good chance he would have an idea who bought them."

"Sounds promising."

"It was, but you saved me a trip."

"Who is he?"

"His name's Travis Parker," Clay said. "He's the latest in a long line of Parker dirtbags. I had more than a few run-ins with his father and his uncles back when I was the sheriff around here, but this one hasn't been in the news as much. That means he's either smarter than his idiot elders, or he's better at what he does."

"And what does he do?"

"If he's like the rest of the Parkers, he's not picky."

I thought about this a moment, then said, "Maybe don't cancel."

Clay looked at me, motioned to the box. "Isn't that what you came for?"

"I'm not so sure," I said. "Something feels wrong about all of this."

"So you still want me to go talk to him?"

"No, I want us both to go talk to him."

"Not a good idea," Clay said. "These people, they don't like strangers."

"But they're okay with ex-lawmen?"

Clay frowned. "Suit yourself, but I don't know what you're hoping to find."

I thought about that and decided I didn't know either. I only knew that something about Lilly's life didn't feel right, and talking to someone who knew her might help bring things into focus. Maybe I was looking for closure, or maybe the more I dug into her life in Beaumont Cove, the longer I could put off saying goodbye.

It was as good of a reason as any.

When I saw Clay's car, I laughed out loud.

"You're kidding," I said. "A Crown Vic?"

"What's wrong with that?"

"Once a cop, always a cop."

"I bought it at auction," he said. "It had a few miles on it, but it was in good shape. Cops take care of their cars."

"My dad had one, too," I said. "No judgment."

I didn't want to admit it, but part of me was happy to see that car, and as we drove north, heading into the hills on the outskirts of town, I couldn't help but smile. There was something comforting about riding in such a familiar vehicle. It made me think of my father, and of long trips reading in the back seat or playing gin rummy with Lilly for pennies while my dad sang along to the oldies station.

The more I remembered, the less I felt like smiling.

I pushed the thoughts of Lilly and my father from my mind, then turned to Clay and said, "Tell me about this guy we're going to see."

"Travis Parker?" Clay shook his head. "I don't know much about him. I remember him when he was a kid. He's stayed out of trouble over the years, and that's something coming from that family."

"Do you think he'll talk to us?"

"Probably not."

I laughed, thinking he was joking, but when he didn't join in, I stopped.

"The Parkers keep to themselves, always have," Clay said. "And that's a good thing. Used to be a time when people went out of their way to avoid them, but that was back when Bob and his brothers ran things. Now, Bob's going on seventy, and both of his brothers are dead. You don't hear much about the family anymore."

"What exactly did they run?"

"Name it," Clay said. "I arrested the youngest brother for selling guns, but that was only part of their setup." He paused, losing himself in the memory. "They were a one-stop shop for whatever you needed. At their peak, they were a distribution hub for cocaine and marijuana coming up from Mexico, but they didn't limit themselves. Everything from drugs and guns to card games and dogfights. If you knew a way to make money, they wanted in on it. The specifics of the job didn't matter."

"What about now?"

"What do you mean?"

"Sounds like that side of the family has come and gone," I said. "You told me you didn't know anything about the guy we're going to see. Maybe he's a new generation of law-abiding Parkers."

Clay laughed.

"Laugh all you want," I said. "But if he was a friend of Lilly's, he has to have a good side. She wouldn't have had anything to do with him if he was trouble."

"You sure about that?"

I started to tell him I was, but before the words were out, I felt a small ping of doubt in the back of my mind. Since she'd left, Lilly had done things I never would've thought possible for her. If she was capable of lying to me, of taking my money and our mother's things, then keeping company with criminals wasn't much of a leap.

"I'm not sure about anything," I said. "If you'd have asked me a year ago, I would've said something different."

Clay adjusted himself in his seat, said, "Can I ask you a question?"

I told him he could.

"What happened between you two?" He glanced over at me, then back at the road. "The fight you two had, it was about more than Mike, wasn't it?"

"She never told you?"

He shook his head. "She talked to Ava, but that woman keeps the things she hears to herself."

I nodded, looked down at my hands folded in my lap, then out the passenger window at the town sliding silently by under the gray-green light of the sky.

I must've been quiet for a long time, because Clay cleared his throat, said, "Hell, forget about it. I don't want to pry."

"It's not that," I said. "It's just that I did something I'm not proud of, and I've never told anyone." I started to say more, but my throat closed on the words, and it took a moment before I could go on. "I did something for her."

"Was it that bad?"

"Who can tell anymore?" I said. "Sometimes it seems like no one knows what's right or what's wrong these days. Everything is just a different shade of gray." I paused. "All I know is that it eats at me, and I can't get away from it."

"We all have regrets."

"I know," I said. "But I'd do it again if I thought it would change things."

Clay waited for me to go on.

Eventually, I did.

"After my dad died, I put all my focus on my work. We had a few cases sitting around, and I dove in, trying to block out reality."

"Makes sense."

"One of the cases was for a small tech company just outside of Colorado Springs. They suspected one of their employees of stealing from them, and they hired me to find proof. It was an easy job. The guy was careless, and he left a trail so obvious that part of me thought he was trying to get caught."

"Was he?"

"No," I said. "He just didn't know what he was doing, and when I confronted him, he was shocked. When I told him how much trouble he was in, he panicked. He gave me this sad story about his wife threatening divorce, and how they'd emptied their kid's college account to cover bills. He claimed the company had canceled his bonus, and they were trying to cheat him out of money they owed him, and on and on."

Clay stayed focused on the road, didn't speak.

"He offered me ten thousand dollars on the spot if I'd look the other way."

"I see."

"I thought if I could get Lilly set up in a different town, far away from Mike, that she could have a different life, and that she'd be safe. Mike was never going to leave her alone, not as long as she was in Manitou, and at the time it seemed like the only way I could protect her."

"So you took the money."

"Without a second thought," I said. "Lilly's safety in exchange for my integrity seemed like a small price to pay. Of course, things didn't turn out like I'd hoped."

"She didn't want the money?"

"No, she took the money," I said. "She even used it to leave town. The problem was that she left town with Mike."

"You're kidding?"

"She wrote me a letter," I said. "She thought they needed a fresh start someplace new where no one knew them. She believed everything would be better between them if they could start over, and she swore she'd pay me back." I paused. "They got married somewhere along the way, and that was it."

Clay didn't say anything, and for a long time we drove in silence.

I could feel him beside me, judging me, and after a while I couldn't take the silence anymore, so I turned to face him and said, "There you go. That's my secret."

"It's not so bad."

"It's the worst thing I've ever done."

Clay laughed, mumbled to himself, "The worst thing you've ever done."

"I traded my beliefs and my self-respect for cash," I said. "You think it's funny?"

"No, Maggie." He turned and looked at me, and for the first time since I'd met him, I saw softness in his eyes. "I think you're very young."

Chapter Twenty-Seven

We drove on.

I watched through the passenger window as the town gave way to empty, windswept fields and rolling hills. Eventually, Clay turned off the highway onto a dirt road that we followed into a forest thick with evergreens and shadows.

"Do you know where you're going?" I asked.

Clay told me he did, and a few minutes later, we pulled through a rusted metal gate and drove down a long weed-covered drive to a wooden cabin half hidden among the pine trees. The cabin was well kept. There was a swing on the porch, and a rock-walled firepit surrounded by Adirondack chairs in the yard. The bushes in front of the house were manicured, and a flood of color spilled from two flower boxes mounted outside the second-floor windows.

Clay parked out front and shut off the engine.

"You sure this is the right place?" I asked. "It looks nice."

"This is the place." He opened the door and stepped out.

I followed.

"They don't know we're coming," he said. "So let me do the talking."

That was fine with me, and I was about to tell him so when the front door opened and a young woman in dirty jeans and a faded Hulk Hogan T-shirt stepped out onto the porch. She had work gloves in one hand, and a metal bucket filled with garden tools in the other. When she saw us, she set the bucket down and walked to the edge of the porch and stood with her hands on her hips, watching us.

Clay moved closer, and I followed.

"We're looking for Travis Parker," he said. "Is he here?"

"Are you a cop?"

"No, ma'am."

The woman sighed and pointed to the side of the house and said, "He's around back. He's supposed to be cleaning out the garden for the winter, but if he's not, you'll probably find him asleep on the hammock. Feel free to wake his lazy ass up if he is."

Clay thanked her, and we made our way around the side of the cabin.

Once we were out of earshot, I asked, "Did you know her?"

Clay shook his head.

If the well-tended front yard had been a surprise, the backyard left me speechless. There was an elevated redwood porch overlooking a large tilled plot of fenced-in earth that I assumed was the garden. A man-made creek snaked along the edge of the yard, ending in a waterfall that dropped into a clear pond filled with koi.

Next to the pond, a low stone bench marked the entrance to a walking path leading into a shaded forest of loblolly pines.

"Are you kidding me?" I asked. "You made these people sound like animals."

Clay frowned. "I guess it's been a while."

I started to ask him exactly how long it'd been when a man stepped out onto the porch and said, "Help you?"

We both turned toward the sound. The man on the porch was tall and rail thin. He wore a loose pair of overalls, no shirt, and every inch of exposed skin was covered in a patchwork of small, random tattoos. He had dark hair and a thin beard, and the skin around his eyes had a blue tint to it, as if he hadn't slept for days.

I leaned closer to Clay. "See, this is more like it."

Clay ignored me and stepped forward. "Travis Parker?"

"That's right."

"We have a couple questions. Do you have a minute?"

Travis walked to the edge of the porch, squinted down at us. "Sheriff Jenkins? Is that you?"

"It's just Clay these days," he said. "Mind if we come up?"

Travis didn't say anything, and it took a moment before I realized he was staring at me. Slowly, I lifted my hand, waved.

"Holy shit." For an instant he seemed to lose his train of thought, but he recovered just as quickly and motioned us up. "Come on around. Stairs are on the side."

We walked to the foot of the steps, and as we started up, Clay looked down at me and whispered, "Remember, let me do the talking."

I rolled my eyes, followed.

When we reached the top, Travis came forward, smiling. He was wiping dirt from his hands with a red bandanna, and when he got close, he slipped the cloth into the back pocket of his overalls and held out his hand. "It's good to see you, Sheriff. How long has it been?"

"Ten years at least," Clay said. "I barely recognize the place."

"And you." He turned to me, his eyes wide. "You don't need an introduction." He held out his hand. "You're Magnolia James. I've heard a lot about you."

I shook his hand. "Maggie."

"Would you two like a beer?" he asked. "Or Patty just made some lemonade."

We told him we were fine, and he led us across the porch to a wrought-iron picnic table surrounded by several metal chairs with thick cushions.

Once we were seated, he turned to me and said, "I'm damn sorry about your sister. She was a sweet girl. I can't believe what happened."

I glanced over at Clay, then back to Travis. "You were friends with her?"

"Through Mike," he said. "We worked together on the boardwalk last spring, and we hit it off. When I heard what he did, I couldn't believe it."

"Really?" I asked. "You knew him, but you couldn't believe it?"

Travis heard the tone in my voice, and his eyes narrowed.

"Because I believed it," I said. "The second I heard, I knew exactly what he'd done."

Travis looked over at Clay, his eyes questioning.

Clay leaned forward. "I think what she's trying to say is that there was a long history of violence with Mike, and—"

"Did you ever see him hit her?" I asked.

"What?" Travis frowned. "No, of course not."

"Never?"

"Never." He paused. "After I heard what happened, I looked back on a few things. There were signs, bruises mostly, but they seemed happy for the most part. Besides, it wasn't any of my business."

"Happy?"

Travis nodded. "On the outside, they got along pretty well. They were always laughing at each other's jokes, affectionate toward one another, that kind of thing."

I listened to his description and tried to ignore the chill in my bones. What he saw between them was the same thing I'd seen before they'd run off. Their relationship looked ideal from the outside, and anyone who met them would've described them as a happy couple. Sure, Lilly was always hiding bruises, but no one would've believed they'd come from Mike.

I wanted to ask more, but before I could, Clay spoke.

"Do you know if Lilly sold any items in the time you knew her?"

Travis seemed to think about it. "Not that I know of."

"Nothing at all?"

"Like what?"

Clay looked at me, nodded.

I'd started a list back at the hotel, but I didn't have it with me, so I went by memory. "A black pearl necklace, some earrings, a diamond engagement ring? She also had an antique broach with an emerald set in the center."

Travis shook his head.

"How about a key?" I asked. "It was silver. She wore it on a chain around—"

"Around her neck," he said. "Yeah, she wore it all the time."

"Do you know what happened to it?"

"I wouldn't know," he said. "I never saw her without it." He pointed back and forth between Clay and me. "Why are you two asking me about this stuff?"

I sat back, letting Clay answer.

"There's no delicate way to put it," he said. "I thought, because of your father, that you might've helped her find a buyer for some of the more valuable items."

"There it is." Travis laughed.

"I didn't intend to—"

"No, I get it," Travis said. "But you've got the wrong Parker. I'm the white sheep of the family, Sheriff. Sorry to disappoint you."

"Had to check," he said. "We appreciate your help."

"Sorry it didn't amount to much."

We all stood, shook, and started toward the steps leading back down to the yard. Halfway there, I stopped and turned around. "You said Mike and Lilly seemed happy together for the most part."

"That's right."

"What did you mean?" I asked. "For the most part?"

Travis shrugged. "They had their arguments, like every couple. I don't know a lot of the details."

"Anything would help," I said. "I'm working in a fog."

"He did mention making her quit her job at the diner, said she'd been flirting with customers. I didn't believe it at the time. Mike had a jealous streak, and he was always suspicious of any man she'd meet. It wasn't until the fight that I started to wonder if there was something to all of it."

"The fight?"

"With the maintenance guy at their apartment," he said. "I guess he'd been sniffing around Lilly, and Mike had to warn him off a couple times, but the guy kept coming back. Mike told me he'd catch him ducking out of sight whenever he was around."

"They knew each other?"

"Yeah, they knew each other," Travis said. "I was over there when the guy got in Mike's face. At that point, Mike didn't have a choice. He had to put a stop to it."

"They got into a physical fight?"

"I don't know that I'd technically call it a fight," Travis said, smiling. "Mike had a hundred pounds on him, easy. Ask Mike about it, he'll tell you all you want to know."

I thanked him again, then turned and started down the stairs.

Clay followed, and we walked back around the cabin to the front. It seemed to take forever to get back to the car, and each step felt heavier than the last. When we were finally in the car and pulling out of the driveway, Clay broke the silence.

"What was that about?"

"I'm not sure," I said. "The maintenance guy at Lilly's apartment lied to me."

Clay seemed to think about this, said, "Do you think he could've taken anything?"

"I don't know."

"You want me to do some digging?"

"Not yet," I said. "I'm going over there tonight. I'll talk to him myself first."

"Are you sure?"

I nodded. "Let's meet for lunch tomorrow. I'll let you know what he says."

Chapter Twenty-Eight

Thomas

Thomas whistled to himself as he carried his radio across the parking lot and into the apartment beneath Lilly's. He set it on the floor, plugged it in, then turned the volume on high before grabbing the paint roller and picking up where he'd left off.

Work went faster with music.

At least that was what his mother used to tell him back when he was so small and she was so big. He used to believe that she knew all the secrets of the world, and that she had every answer he'd ever need. Eventually, he'd learned that she didn't know much about anything, but she had been right about music.

Thomas pushed the roller through the paint tray, then stepped up to the wall and spun on his heels, sending a spray of eggshell across the drop cloth.

He barely noticed.

He hummed along to the radio and ran the roller over the wall in the familiar W pattern, and he didn't mind the repetitiveness of the job, or that the smell of paint fumes made him dizzy and sometimes gave him a headache.

Because today, life was beautiful.

It wasn't because he'd finally had the idea to bring his radio along with him while he worked, or because this was the last building he had to repaint. No, life was beautiful because no matter how bad things seem, there was always a surprise waiting right around the corner. Once you accepted that things were a certain way, something would always happen to change everything. For him, someone came back in his life, wrapped her arms around him, and reminded him of all the beautiful possibilities to come.

Yes, life was beautiful indeed.

In no time, Thomas finished the big wall in the living room, and he was about to start on the next when he felt a hand on his arm and spun around, startled.

Maggie was next to him.

She was saying something, but Thomas couldn't hear her, so he set the roller in the paint tray, then reached for the radio and turned the volume down.

"Sorry, I didn't hear you."

"How could you?" Maggie said. "Classical music?"

"That's right." Thomas wiped his hands on his pants. "Do you like it?"

"No."

"Oh."

"Listen," she said. "I hate to bug you, but would you mind letting me in upstairs? I wanted to start packing some of Lilly's things, and I thought I'd take another look to see if I could find her necklace."

"No problem." Thomas took the master key ring from his pocket and motioned toward the door. "After you."

He followed her outside and up the steps. When they reached Lilly's apartment, Thomas unlocked the door and went inside. He held the door for her.

"Thank you." She stepped inside, then turned to face him. "I don't know how long I'll be here, but I'll try not to bother you."

"You couldn't bother me," he said, smiling. "Matter of fact, if you'd like some company, I'd be happy to help. I'm batting a thousand after finding the box. I could try my luck with her necklace."

"I don't want to pull you away," she said. "You're busy."

"It can wait," he said. "This is the last building I have to do, so I'm all yours if you'll have me."

He gave her his best smile, but she didn't smile back.

"Thanks," she said. "But I think I'll go it alone this time."

Thomas felt a weight form in the center of his chest, pulling him down. He ignored it the best he could. "I understand."

He kept his voice light, casual. "If you change your mind, I'll be right downstairs."

He turned away, forcing himself to leave. He would give her some time alone, then he'd come back up to check on her, and to see how she was doing. Maybe after some time alone, she'd change her mind and want company.

Thomas stopped on the landing outside the apartment. When he turned back, she was standing in the doorway. He felt his breath catch, and he made a small croaking sound that surprised them both.

"Are you okay?"

Thomas felt himself blush, and he cleared his throat before he spoke. "I'm sorry. Seeing you standing there took me by surprise. It was just so familiar."

Maggie frowned. "Thomas, can I ask you something?"

"Anything."

"Why did you lie to me about knowing Mike?"

Thomas felt his chest tighten. "Lie to you?"

"I asked if you knew Mike, and you told me you didn't," she said. "You said you never spoke to him."

"I didn't—" His throat closed over the words. "I guess I meant that I didn't know him. I barely—"

"Tell me about the fight."

"The fight?"

"You started a fight with him," she said.

"Who told you about—"

Then, all at once, he understood.

Lilly had written about it in her diary.

Now her sister stood there accusing him of lying when she was the one who had lied to him. The notebook hadn't been blank. She just didn't want him to know what Lilly had written about him. Did she want to use it against him?

Was that her plan?

Thomas felt the tightness in his chest turn hot and burn through him.

He wanted to scream at her, make her tell him what Lilly had written, and he had to force himself to keep from grabbing her and shaking her until she gave in to him.

"You lied to me," she said. "Why would you do that?"

Thomas closed his eyes and tried to center himself.

"Are you going to answer me?"

Thomas took a deep breath and turned toward the window, buying time. When he felt under control, he whispered, "The fight with Mike. It wasn't my finest hour."

"What happened?"

"It was Lilly. She had bruises." He touched his lip, his cheek. "I knew what he did to her, and I thought I could help."

"By starting a fight?"

"I didn't want to fight him," he said. "I wanted to talk to him. I wanted him to know that I knew what he'd done, and that I was watching him, but when I confronted him about it, things got out of hand. He got angry, and—"

"How often did you talk to Lilly?"

"Only a few times," he said. "I told you, I fixed a light switch for her once, and I'd see her around the complex. She kept to herself."

"You didn't keep coming by, trying to talk to her?"

"I'd say hello if I saw her." Thomas frowned. "I don't understand what—"

"How about Mike?"

"I never saw him."

"Never?"

"He worked most days," Thomas said. "At night he'd go to the Royale."

"The Royale?"

"It's a bar down by the arcade."

"Lilly didn't go with him?"

"Not that I know of," he said. "She rarely left her apartment."

"And you didn't go over when he was gone? You didn't follow her around?"

"Follow her around?" Thomas shook his head. "I tried to keep my distance."

"Why?"

"Because she was married, and . . ." Thomas lifted a hand, stopping himself. "Forget it. None of that's important, not anymore."

"What were you going to say?"

Thomas let the silence grow, then said, "I don't know that you want to hear it."

"Now you have to tell me."

"Maggie, your sister was lonely," he said. "She didn't have any friends that I saw, only Mike. At first I'd talk to her when I'd run into her, but sometimes she'd see me working outside, and she'd come out. I didn't mind at first, but after a while I started to worry that she was getting the wrong idea, and—"

"What idea is that?"

"It doesn't matter," he said. "It was probably nothing."

"Are you telling me Lilly wanted more from you than friendship?"

"I don't feel comfortable saying that."

"Then what are you saying?"

"I'm saying she was lonely," he said. "That's all."

Maggie stared at him, her eyes sharp.

Thomas struggled to read her expression, but she showed nothing. Her face was cold and empty, and he didn't like that, so he kept talking, hoping to get back to the place they were before she asked about Mike.

"I'm sorry I lied to you," he said. "Truth is I was embarrassed."

"Because Mike beat you up?"

"No." Her words had hit him like a punch to the chest, and once again he felt his temper flare. "I was embarrassed because I knew what was going on with them, and I couldn't help her."

The look on Maggie's face softened, and Thomas knew he'd said the right thing.

"I get it," Maggie said. "I couldn't help her either."

"But I should've told you the truth," he said. "I hope you're not too angry."

"No, I think I understand now."

Thomas felt the tension slowly drain away. He knew he'd come close to screwing up, but, like always, he'd managed to pull out of the nosedive and land safe and soft in a field of flowers. The relief he felt glowed inside of him, and for a while all he could do was stand in the doorway and stare at Maggie and smile.

This time, she smiled back. "I should get to work."

"Right," he said. "Me too. If you change your mind about needing help, I'll be downstairs."

She thanked him and started to close the door.

"I'll come up and check on you in a while, if you don't—"

The door closed, and he heard the lock click into place.

Thomas stood outside the door a moment longer before going back down the stairs to the apartment below. He turned his radio on, and picked up the roller brush. Soon, he was lost again in the work. Eventually thoughts of Maggie crawled through the cracks of his concentration, and it wasn't long before she was all he could think about.

He glanced at his watch.

Only fifteen minutes had gone by.

He told himself he'd give her fifteen more minutes and then he'd go up and check on her. He hoped by then she'd be tired of being alone and would want his company.

Life really was beautiful.

When the fifteen minutes had passed, Thomas climbed the stairs to the apartment and knocked on the door.

There was no answer.

He tried again before letting himself in with the master key.

The apartment was empty.

Maggie was gone.

Chapter Twenty-Nine

MAGNOLIA

It was past noon, and the Mercury Café was only half-full when I walked in.

The sign by the hostess podium told me to seat myself, so I stood at the entrance and looked around for Clay. Three men in overalls sat at the dining counter to my right, all eating burgers and staring up at the local news on a television mounted on the wall. An older waitress stood behind the counter, filling saltshakers, and a teenage girl in a dirty white apron carried a tray of dishes toward the kitchen. To my left, several red leather booths ran along the wall, and I scanned each one until I saw Clay.

Ava was with him, sitting on the same side of the booth.

I started toward them.

As I got close, Clay looked up and said, "There she is. We thought you got lost." He nodded to the woman next to him. "You've met Ava."

I told him I had, then slid into the booth across from them. "How's my reading coming?" I asked. "Did you see anything interesting after I left?"

"I did," she said. "Why don't you stop in later, and we'll discuss."

"You and I need to have a talk about that."

Ava frowned, turned to Clay. "You told her?"

"She's not a damn tourist, Ava. You shouldn't do that kind of thing."

"I'm not hurting anyone."

"It's dishonest."

"It's framing a situation in a new light to see it in a different way." She looked at me. "Are you upset with me, Magnolia?"

I thought about it and realized I wasn't, and I told her so.

"See?" she said to Clay. "Not only is she not upset, but I bet if you asked her, she'd tell you she enjoyed her visit."

"She was stoned," he said. "Again, thanks to you."

"She's an adult. I didn't twist her arm."

"Not the point."

"Oh hell, Clayton. You're just jealous." Ava leaned across the table, put a hand on my arm. "Don't listen to him. If you want to come back, you're always welcome."

I tried not to smile, and failed.

"Is something funny?"

“I’m sorry,” I said. “I was just wondering how long you two were married.”

“Were married?” Ava turned and glared at Clay. “What did you tell her?”

Clay shrugged.

Ava shook her head, faced me. “We’ll be married twenty years this April.”

“You’re still married?”

“For now at least.” Ava looked at Clay. “Why would you lie to her like that?”

“A man can dream.”

“You keep dreaming, old man. One of these days I’m going to bury you upside down in a pine box. Then we’ll see how funny you think it—”

There was a loud crash across the diner, and the sound of glass shattering.

We all turned.

The teenage girl in the dirty apron was standing beside the counter, a tray of broken plates and glasses at her feet. She stood perfectly still with her hands covering her mouth. She was staring at us.

No, she was staring at me.

“Oh no.” Ava pushed Clay’s arm. “Let me out.”

Clay stood and Ava slid out of the booth. She crossed the diner and took the girl by the arm, leading her away. The older waitress came out from behind the counter and began picking up the broken glass. As she worked, I saw her glance up at me, but when I met her eyes, she looked away.

Clay sat down across from me.

"What was that about?" I asked.

"That's Eloise," he said.

"Is she okay?"

"Hard to tell sometimes," he said. "She had an accident a few years ago. Hasn't been the same since."

"What kind of accident?"

"She was swimming with some friends and got caught in a riptide," he said. "By the time we got to her, she wasn't breathing. We managed to bring her back, but she'd been gone for several minutes."

"Brain damage?"

"No, she's as quick as she ever was. She's just different now."

"Different how?"

Clay reached for a half-filled coffee cup on the table and took a drink. When he set it down, I could tell he was considering his words.

"She sees things," he said. "Or at least she says she does."

"What kind of things?"

"I really wouldn't know," he said. "I'd tell you to ask her, but from her reaction, I'd say she's not ready to talk to you yet."

"Me? What do I have to do with—" I stopped, beginning to understand. "This is where Lilly worked."

Clay nodded, took another drink.

Slowly, I turned and looked around the diner. There were now three waitresses standing behind the counter, all of them pretending to not look at me.

"I think it's time I leave," I said. "Maybe next time we meet somewhere else?"

"Understood," he said. "But first tell me what happened with the maintenance guy. Did he come clean?"

"Yes and no. He admitted to fighting with Mike, but tried to play it off like he was trying to help Lilly." I shook my head. "He's lying about something, but I don't what it is yet. The guy is just off. Are you still willing to do some digging?"

"Consider it done."

"I'm going out to talk to Mike again this afternoon," I said. "I want to hear his side of what happened, because Thomas's story doesn't add up."

"You got a ride?"

"I was going to take a cab."

"All the way there and back?" Clay asked. "That's going to cost you a fortune."

"No choice."

Clay frowned. "Do you have a license?"

I told him I did.

He reached into his pocket and took out his keys and handed them to me over the table. "Just don't crash into anything."

"Are you sure?"

"Some reason I shouldn't be?"

I took the keys before he could change his mind. "I'll fill the tank."

"Yes, you will, and Maggie—"

He was about to say something else, but before he could, Ava was back. She slid in beside him and said, "That girl can be so sensitive at times, but it's all cleared up."

"I'm leaving anyway." I held up the keys. "Thanks again."

"Don't mention it," Clay said. "And I'll let you know what I find when you get back. It shouldn't take too long."

"Can I expect you later?" Ava asked. "I think you'll like what I have to say."

"I'm not sure about tonight," I said. "But I'll come by before I leave town."

She smiled to herself. "If you leave town."

"What?"

"Never mind." She waved me off. "Stop by anytime. I'll be there."

As I walked out, I made a point of not looking at the waitresses behind the counter, and when I reached the door, I thought I'd made it. But then I heard a small voice behind me, calling me.

"Miss?"

I turned.

The young girl in the dirty apron was coming toward me, slowly. She stopped a few feet away, scanning my face, silent.

I didn't know what to say to her, so I kept it simple.

"Eloise, right?"

She smiled, nodded.

"Are you okay?" I asked.

She didn't say anything, and her smile didn't fade.

I glanced back toward the booth where Clay and Ava were sitting, but they were out of my line of sight. I turned back, planning on telling the girl that I had to go, but before I could, she stepped in and wrapped her arms around me, squeezing hard.

Slowly, I hugged her back.

When we finally broke, I looked up and saw the other waitresses standing behind her. Each of them came forward, one at a time, and hugged me.

None of us said a word.

Chapter Thirty

I'd learned to drive in a Crown Vic, but it had been a while, and at first I took it slow. But when I turned onto the highway, I pushed the pedal to the floor, watched the needle jump, and all at once I was seventeen again.

It didn't take long to get to the Beaumont County jail. I checked in at the gate, then pulled into the parking lot. Security didn't go as fast without Sheriff Parks by my side, but eventually I made it through and took a seat in the waiting room.

On the television, a woman with a microphone was once again making a young girl cry in front of a studio audience.

Eventually they called my name, and I followed a guard through the large metal door to a familiar dark room. I sat at the same half cubicle I'd sat at the last time and watched through the same scratched glass as the same guard led Mike into the room.

At first, I thought they'd brought the wrong person.

I barely recognized him.

Mike's head was shaved bald, and his left forearm was in a blue cast. There were bruises around both his eyes, and when he sat down across from me and reached for the phone, he smiled, revealing a gap.

I picked up on my end and said, "Enjoying your time inside?"

"Fuck you, Mags," he said. "Did you find out who killed your sister?"

"You know . . ." I paused. "I can't say that I've looked."

"Of course you didn't." He shook his head. "I guess we don't have anything to talk about."

"In a hurry to get back to your cell?"

I waited.

Mike frowned. "If you're not here to help me, then what do you want?"

"I met a friend of yours," I said. "Works at your old apartment. Thomas?"

"A friend of mine?" He smiled. "That's funny."

"Yeah, he didn't think much of you either," I said. "But he told me an interesting story about you, and about how he tried to keep you from beating up Lilly."

Mike didn't say anything, so I decided to push.

"According to him, Lilly had a bit of a thing for him," I said. "He told me she would follow him around while he was working around the place, and—"

"Bullshit."

"Yeah, that's what I thought, too," I said. "That doesn't sound like Lilly to me."

"She told me he creeped her out," Mike said. "I had to go over there and tell him to back off."

"Did he back off?"

"Obviously not," Mike said. "There's something wrong with that guy."

"How so?"

"Have you met him?"

"He helped me find the box you and Lilly took."

Mike paused. "He was in my apartment?"

I smiled. "Going through all your things."

Mike's jaw twitched, and he looked away.

I felt a delicious sting of joy, and I decided to push. "He seemed convinced there was something between him and Lilly. You don't think he's telling the truth and you just missed it, do you?"

I expected Mike to blow up, or to at least yell at me, but he didn't. Instead, he sat quietly with the phone pressed to his ear, and he didn't say anything.

"You're not sure, are you?"

"I'm sure," he said. "Of course I'm sure."

I heard doubt in his voice.

"But?"

Mike looked away, frowned. "He had her fucking underwear, Maggie."

"What?"

"Did you even read what I told the cops that night?"

I told him I hadn't.

"He left her a note," Mike said. "It said something about what they had together. How they would fuck, and how it had to end. He'd pinned it to a pair of her underwear, said she'd left them at his place."

"And you found them?"

"On our doorknob," he said. "He hung them there, and I found them that night when I got home."

I let this sink in, thinking about Mike's reaction to finding the note pinned to Lilly's underwear. It was too much to imagine, and I pushed the thought away.

"What happened to the note?"

"The cops said they never found one."

"So they didn't believe you?"

Mike smirked at me. "Look around. What do you think?"

I studied him, trying to decide if he was telling the truth. It was my habit to always assume Mike was lying, but this time it wasn't so easy. If there had been a note, the cops would've found it, so why did a part of me believe him?

"Do you think it's still in the apartment?"

"How the hell would I know?" he asked. "You'd have to go look."

He was right, I would.

Behind him, the guard said, "Finish up."

"Got to go, Mags. There's a hell of a poker game going on, and I'm missing it."

"Right," I said. "One last thing, her necklace with the key. What happened to it?"

"She never took it off, you know that." The guard stepped closer, and Mike said, "Sorry, Mags, gotta run."

I sat and watched as he hung up the phone, and I didn't move until he'd walked out and I was alone.

Before I left the jail, I called Clay's office, hoping I'd catch him.

He answered on the second ring.

"What did you find out?" he asked.

I told him everything Mike had said. When I mentioned the underwear and the note, Clay interrupted. "She was sleeping with him?"

"No."

"Then you think Mike is lying?"

"It's funny," I said, "but I don't."

"So you don't think she was sleeping with him?"

"I know she wasn't."

"How do you know?"

"Because I know Lilly," I said. "That's not her."

Clay grunted, and I could tell he wasn't sold.

"I'm going back to her apartment," I said. "I'm going to tear the place apart. If there was a note, I'm going to find it."

"You should call the sheriff, see if he'll send one of his deputies along."

"You think that's necessary?"

"What I've found so far doesn't paint this guy in the best light."

I stayed quiet, waiting for him to go on.

"Turns out, our friend spent a few years in Archway Psychiatric Hospital. They had him labeled as a violent offender, and the records are sealed, so I'm guessing he was underage. I haven't found out what he did yet, but I'll get the records eventually." He paused. "Whatever he did, they locked him up tight over it."

"Are you sure about all of this?"

"Of course I'm sure," Clay said. "Give me a day or two, and I'll have more details for you. Until then, I'd feel better if you stayed clear of him."

"I'm heading over there now," I said. "I want to look for that note."

Clay was quiet for a moment, then said, "At least don't go alone."

"You're overreacting."

"Then consider it a favor," he said. "Repayment for using my car."

"Seriously?"

"Seriously."

I sighed. "Fine, I'll call Parks."

Clay was satisfied, and after we hung up, I walked back to the car in the parking lot and got in. I had my phone in my hand, and I pulled up the number for the sheriff's department, but I didn't dial. It didn't seem right bothering the sheriff, and for a moment I almost abandoned the idea, despite telling Clay I would.

In the end, I made the call.

I had to.

I'd given my word.

Chapter Thirty-One

The woman who answered the phone at the sheriff's office sounded surprised someone was calling. I told her my name, then asked if Sheriff Parks was around. She told me he was in a meeting but she could take a message.

I started to tell her I'd call back, but before I could, she said, "Oh, he just stepped out. Hang on a sec."

The line clicked, and I waited.

When Sheriff Parks picked up, he sounded hurried. "Miss James?"

"Sheriff," I said. "Sorry to bother you."

"Not a bother, just give me one minute." I listened as he shuffled something on the line, then he said, "All right, how can I help?"

"I have a couple questions if you've got time."

"I'll answer what I can."

"The night my sister died, Mike mentioned finding some kind of note."

"Pinned to a pair of Lilly's undergarments, if I remember correctly."

"That's right."

"He mentioned that more than a few times after we arrested him," Parks said. "He claimed Thomas and your sister were having some kind of affair behind his back, but we didn't find a note, and Thomas denied anything ever happened between them."

"I'd like to look again," I said. "In case your guys missed it."

"That's up to you, but I can assure you we were thorough."

"I'd feel better if I looked myself. Mike was adamant about it."

"I understand," he said. "But even if you were to find a note, it's not going to change anything. It'll only confirm his motivation."

"I know."

Parks paused. "Can I ask your interest in this note? You don't think Lilly and—"

"No, I don't."

"I'd have to say, I've known guys over the years who were punching above their weight class, but that would've been one for the record books."

I let the comment pass, then said, "I don't know too much about Thomas. What can you tell me about him?"

"Keeps to himself," Parks said. "Quiet, hardworking, a bit scatterbrained. He can be awkward around other people, but seems to do fine on his own. Why do you ask?"

"Do you know why he was hospitalized?"

"How'd you hear about that?"

"Is that important?"

Parks made a scoffing sound, mumbled, "Clay Jenkins."

It wasn't a question, so I ignored it.

"I've been trying to piece together what happened leading up to Lilly's death," I said. "I thought if I had a better picture of her life, it would be easier for me to come to terms with what happened."

"I suppose I can understand."

"But when I started digging, a few things didn't add up."

"And Thomas was one of them?"

"He lied to me," I said. "He told me he never talked with Mike, and that he only saw Lilly a couple times around the apartments."

"Sounds about right," Parks said. "That matches what he told us."

"Then I met a friend of Mike's," I said. "A man named Travis Parker."

"Now, how the hell did you find—" He stopped, exhaled, long and slow. "Go on."

"Mike and Thomas got in a fight," I said. "According to Travis, Thomas confronted Mike about Lilly, and Mike beat him up over it. He said it was bad, and that Mike humiliated him."

"Travis knew this how?"

"He was there, and he witnessed the entire thing," I said. "And when I asked Thomas about it, he reluctantly confessed."

"You confronted Thomas about this?"

"He told me he was trying to help Lilly," I said. "He also claimed that Lilly was interested in him romantically, and that she wouldn't leave him alone. He said she'd follow him around while he was trying to work." I paused. "Pushing herself on him."

Parks laughed out loud. "I can't imagine that's true."

"It's not true," I said. "Nothing he told me was true."

Parks hesitated. "Well, like I said, Thomas keeps to himself. He never goes out, and he doesn't have any friends in town that I know of, so he can be awkward around people. Maybe these little white lies are his way of trying to fit in. I'm sure—"

"What if there was a note, Sheriff?"

"There wasn't."

"But what if there was?" I asked. "If he was lying about Lilly and about getting into a fight, it's possible he's lying about planting a note for Mike to find."

"Why would he want to do that?"

"If Travis was right, and Mike humiliated him, and Lilly rejected him . . ." I paused. "How do you think those things would affect a quiet, awkward loner who keeps to himself? Especially if you look at his history?"

"You're saying Thomas wrote the note as a catalyst?"

"I'm saying there are questions."

"Questions, and no proof."

"Look at everyone involved and where they are now," I said. "Lilly is gone, Mike is in jail, probably for the rest of his life, and Thomas . . ."

"Thomas is happy at home." Parks hesitated. "It's thin, Miss James."

"I know."

"If we'd found the note, then maybe—"

"There was a note," I said. "I can feel it."

"And that's why you'd like to look for yourself," he said. "Well, keep me posted."

"That brings me to why I called."

"You mean it wasn't to bounce your theory off a seasoned and professional law enforcement officer?"

I laughed. "A friend wanted me to ask a favor."

"Let's hear it."

"My friend is concerned, given Thomas's history and the possibility of him being involved in all of this, that it's not safe to go back to Lilly's apartment alone."

"I see."

"I told him he was overreacting, but—"

"You'd like me to come along?"

"I'm on my way there now," I said. "But if you don't have the time, I'm sure it'll be fine if I go alone."

Parks was quiet for a moment, then he sighed and said, "Hang on a sec."

The line clicked, and I waited, listening to a Muzak version of "Let It Be" in one ear, and the low drone of the tires humming along the highway in the other. After about thirty seconds, Parks was back.

"You're in luck," he said. "I've been meaning to stop by the Orion and have a talk with Thomas. Something unrelated. How about I meet you there in ten minutes?"

"I'm further out than that," I said. "But I'll be right behind you."

"Then I'll see you when you get there. Goodbye, Miss James."

He hung up, and I slid the phone into my pocket.

Outside, the sun was starting to set, casting long shadows behind me.

I sped up, driving toward the sea under a burning red sky.

PART THREE

Chapter Thirty-Two

Thomas

Thomas hung up the phone and leaned back in the chair. He took the Beaumont Cove snow globe off the desk, shook it, absently running his thumb over the surface of the thick glass. As always, the miniature town surrounded by white both calmed and enchanted him, and he stared at it for a long time, shaking it again and again.

He was going to have company tomorrow.

The rental company had called to tell him that they'd arranged for two insurance adjusters to come by and inspect the property for any damage incurred during the year. Thomas had tried to tell them that he had taken care of all the repairs, and that there was no reason to send anyone out, but they gave him no choice.

On one level, he knew it wasn't a big deal. He'd grown spoiled having the place all to himself, even though he knew it wouldn't last. Eventually, the outside world would slither its way in, and he'd be forced to deal with the stink of other people. He'd prepared himself for that certainty come summer, but he should've known there would be smaller disturbances scattered here and there throughout the off-season.

Tomorrow was just one of them.

As Thomas stared at the snow globe, he pictured what would happen if the adjusters found something wrong, and the rental company called in contractors to do repairs. He imagined an entire crew of workmen, loud and intrusive, crawling over his buildings like maggots, ripping and tearing.

The more he thought about it, the more the tension inside of him grew. He bit down hard, grinding his teeth together until his jaw ached, but what he really wanted to do was scream. It seemed like it would help to open his mouth and let out one earsplitting, primal roar, releasing all his frustration and anger into the world.

What would it hurt?

He was still considering it when there was a knock at the office door.

Thomas sat up, listened.

A moment later, whoever it was knocked again.

Thomas got up and crossed the room to the window. He carried the snow globe with him, and he moved it from one hand to the other as he split the blinds with two fingers and looked out.

The sheriff's cruiser was parked in the lot.

Thomas frowned, then went to the door, unlocked the bolt, and pulled it open.

Sheriff Parks smiled down at him. "Good evening, Thomas," he said. "Hope I'm not disturbing you."

"Not at all."

"I tried your apartment, but when you weren't there, I figured I'd check here."

"I was on the phone with the rental company," he said. "They're sending an insurance adjuster out tomorrow."

"Damage from the storm?"

"Yeah, but it's nothing I can't handle."

"Not a bad idea to let them check," he said. "Speaking of, you got a minute?"

"If you're here to remind me about my appointment with Dr. Riley, there's no need," he said. "It's in my calendar."

"You got me." Parks smiled. "I was driving by and thought about it, and I figured I'd pop on in and remind you. Should've known you'd be on top of it."

"I am."

"That's good." Parks stepped into the doorway, and Thomas reluctantly moved aside, letting him in. "How are things going after all the excitement?"

"It's been peaceful."

"No new tenants?"

"Just me."

"Sounds lonely." He moved slowly around the room, scanning the walls and the furniture. "You don't see anyone at all?"

"Lilly's sister comes by once in a while."

Parks frowned. "That poor kid, losing a twin like that."

Thomas didn't say anything.

"She must be tough as nails to handle all of this on her own," Parks said. "Both her parents gone, now her sister. Have you had a chance to talk to her?"

"Sure," Thomas said. "I helped her find some of her sister's things."

"Is that right?"

"She was looking for a jewelry box that belonged to her mother, and she couldn't find it anywhere. She asked for my help, and I found it." Thomas beamed, the memory buzzing through him. "She was so happy, she kissed me."

"You don't say?"

"On the cheek," Thomas said, basking in the joy of the lie. "She was very happy."

Sheriff Parks laughed. "Sure sounds like it." He turned away, glancing around the room. "It must be strange seeing her here, with everything that happened."

"It was at first," he said. "But she's not at all like Lilly."

"Is that right?"

"It's like you said, she's tougher than Lilly, and she doesn't act the same."

"How so?"

"You can just tell. She'd never be with someone who treated her badly."

"You mean like Mike?"

Thomas nodded. "Lilly didn't think she deserved to be treated better, but Maggie's not like that, she knows she deserves better."

"Maybe someone like you?"

Thomas flushed and looked away, but the idea glowed inside of him.

"Sorry, Tom. I didn't mean to embarrass you."

"You didn't, I just—"

"I know," Parks said. "It's a dumb idea."

Thomas looked up at him. "What?"

"You and Maggie together. It would never work."

"Why not?" He heard the edge of desperation in his voice, and he did his best to push it down. "We get along really well."

"That may be," Parks said. "But I don't think she trusts you, Tom."

Thomas heard the words and felt the air rush from his lungs. He wanted to argue, but his throat closed and nothing came out.

"I wouldn't take it personally," Parks said. "Considering what she's—"

"Why doesn't she trust me?" he asked. "I haven't done anything to make her not trust me. I've done everything right."

"Hey, it's okay."

"I've done everything right," he said. "You're wrong."

"Thomas."

"No," he said. "She trusts me. I helped her find that box, and I—"

"Tom."

Sheriff Parks's voice was loud, and Thomas stopped. He could feel his pulse pounding behind his ears, and all the muscles in his body ached with the tension. He told himself Parks didn't know what he was talking about, that Parks didn't know Maggie like he did, and that he had no idea how she felt about him. But this time, it didn't make him feel better.

"Listen," Parks said. "I didn't want to come here and upset you, but I—"

"I'm not upset," he said. "I just don't think you know what you're talking about. We've become friends, good friends, and she's been relying on me to—"

"Tom." Parks held up his hands, stopping him. "I'm going to need you to calm down. Can you do that for me?"

Thomas paused, took a deep breath, nodded.

"Thank you." He spoke slowly. "Now, if you'll let me explain."

Again, Thomas nodded.

"I said what I said because of something she mentioned earlier." Parks folded his arms across his chest. "Apparently, the night Lilly died, there was a note."

Thomas didn't look up. "A note?"

"She seems to believe that you left a note for Mike to find, and that note is what set him off, and that was why he killed Lilly."

"That's not true, I—"

"It doesn't matter if it's true or not," Parks said. "If she believes it, even a little bit, you can understand why she doesn't trust you."

"No." Thomas shook his head, looked away. "No, no, no."

"She asked me to look into it, and I told her I would, so—"

"Look into it?" Thomas turned on him, and all at once, the air in the room grew thick. He felt the darkness fade in, and he struggled to push it back. "That's why you're here?"

"I'll start by taking another look inside Lilly's apartment," Parks said. "If you can get me the key, I'd appreciate it."

"Didn't you guys already go through her place?" Thomas asked. "You didn't find a note the first time, so why check again?"

"Sometimes you overlook things. It's rare, but it happens." He paused. "The key, Tom?"

Thomas motioned toward the desk. "Top drawer, but you're not going to find a note, I promise you."

Sheriff Parks froze, looked back at him. "What makes you say that?"

"Because," Thomas said, suddenly realizing how he sounded, "there isn't a note to find. At least not one that I wrote."

Parks nodded, moved toward the desk.

Thomas glanced down at the snow globe in his hand, shook it, watched the snow swirl around the tiny cliffs and Ferris wheel. He tried to think of anything he might've forgotten, or that might point back to him, but there was nothing. He didn't think he had anything to worry about, but if the sheriff was going to look over everything again, there was always the possibility he'd find something.

"Top drawer, you said?"

"It's a key ring," Thomas said. "Should be on top."

"I'm not seeing it."

Thomas came around the desk, and as he approached the sheriff, the darkness swelled in his mind, hungry and unstoppable. It came quickly, rolling over him, and pulling him deeper into the shadows. He never had a chance to stop it.

Thomas saw the keys sitting on the desk, and he pointed them out.

Parks laughed, said, "If they'd been a snake."

Thomas smiled at the joke, then stepped in, raised his arm, and brought the snow globe down hard against the back of Parks's skull. There was a wet, cracking sound, and the sheriff's knees buckled. He dropped hard, his jaw slamming against the desktop. Then he slipped to the side, and landed on his back. His eyes turning over white.

Thomas fell on him.

And he watched, as if through a stranger's eyes, as the snow globe came down, again and again, releasing all his frustration and anger in a crimson shower of blood and bone.

Chapter Thirty-Three

When it was over, Thomas stood and stared at the snow globe in his hand. There were several strands of hair stuck in a thin crack that ran along the hard plastic base. At the end of the hair, dangling like a small pink spider, was a torn chunk of scalp.

The glass globe, scratched and smeared red, was unbroken.

He set the snow globe on the desk, then crouched over Sheriff Parks. A pool of blood was spreading under him, surrounding his head and sinking into the carpet.

Thomas stood and looked around the office.

He spotted the roll of paper towels mounted on the wall next to the coffee maker. He took the entire roll and began wrapping the sheriff's skull. The blood soaked through the towels immediately, but he kept going, and by the time he'd used them all, the blood had stopped spreading.

Thomas stepped back, head cocked, studying his handiwork.

The sheriff's head, cocooned in white, made him think of a snowman dressed in a bloody khaki-and-brown shirt with a crooked gold badge. Thomas felt himself smile, but he turned away, pushing the image out of his head.

Now he had work to do.

If anyone saw Parks like this, they wouldn't see the humor in it the way he did, and he wouldn't be able to explain. He remembered what it was like in the hospital, sitting across from his doctors as they scribbled in their notebooks and asked all the wrong questions.

It didn't matter how it made him feel.

It only mattered that it happened.

Thomas felt his chest tighten when he thought about the hospital. If he was caught, they would send him back, and this time he would never get out again.

He couldn't allow that.

Getting rid of the body would be the hard part. Once that was done, he would replace the carpet. There were remnants in one of the back closets, and it would be easy to cut the ruined section out. After that, he'd need to scrub the walls and the furniture with bleach water, and then he would wait. Eventually, they'd find the body, and there would be an investigation, but no one would have any reason to suspect him. They might come by and ask if he knew anything, but he could handle their questions.

And then it would pass, like it'd never happened.

But first, the body had to go, and he thought he knew how.

Thomas moved the chair from behind the desk, then reached down and grabbed the sheriff's legs. He dragged him a few feet, but the carpet was pulling the paper towels away from his skull, so he went around and picked him up by his shoulders. This wasn't as easy, and by the time he got close to the door, the front of his shirt was soaked through with blood, but the paper towels stayed in place.

Thomas lowered the sheriff's body to the floor. Then he stood, stretching the aches and cramps from his lower back, and reached for the doorknob.

When he opened the door, he froze.

Maggie was standing outside, one hand raised as if to knock.

There was a moment, before the chaos began, when neither of them moved. In that brief blink of time, Maggie looked almost amused. Her eyes went wide, and a thin, startled smile flashed across her lips. In a different situation she might've put a hand to her chest and laughed.

But then she saw the blood.

Every feature on Maggie's face seemed to melt, and her eyes darted past him to the sheriff's body lying on the floor. Her hands went to her mouth, and Thomas knew what was coming.

Before she could make a sound, he reached out, grabbing a fistful of hair at the back of her head with one hand, and pressing his other hand flat against her mouth. He pulled her into the office, lifting her off her feet, and kicked the door closed.

———

Thomas leaned Sheriff Parks against the side of the cruiser, then walked around the building to the equipment shed and took the red gas can from inside. It was full, and he was glad. He would need it all.

When he got back to the cruiser, he searched Parks's pockets for his keys, then he unlocked the trunk. Inside were several black cases, a bright-orange vest, traffic cones, road flares, a flashlight, a fire extinguisher, and a spike strip strapped to the lid with Velcro.

He put the gas can inside, and closed the trunk.

Then he unlocked the rear door.

It took several tries, lifting and pushing, until he was able to roll the sheriff into the back seat. When he finished, he leaned all his weight against the cruiser, feeling his heart beating hard, and tried to catch his breath. He closed his eyes and saw a garden of black flowers bloom in his vision, and for an instant, he thought he might pass out.

But he didn't.

Eventually, the feeling passed, and Thomas stepped back. He looked down at Sheriff Parks, then leaned forward and took the handcuffs and gun from his belt. The gun felt heavy and awkward in his hand, and he didn't like it. He'd never fired a weapon in his life, and he hoped to keep it that way, but he knew that might not be possible.

Thomas stepped back and closed the rear door. He glanced down at the gun in his hand, took a deep breath, preparing himself for what had to come next, and then started back toward the office.

When he went inside, Maggie was where he'd left her, sitting on the floor by the desk, her hands bound with the lamp cord, a strip of duct tape over her mouth. Her eyes followed him as he crossed the room toward her, but she didn't make a sound.

Thomas knelt in front of her with the gun. He wanted to make sure she saw it, hoping that would be enough to keep her from trying anything that would make what he had to do next any more difficult than it needed to be.

"We're going for a ride," he said. "Please don't make me kill you."

Maggie shook her head, and Thomas felt a twinge of relief. But then he noticed her eyes and their complete lack of fear, and he frowned.

"I don't want to hurt you," he said, "but I will. Do you understand?"

She nodded.

"Are you going to cooperate?"

There was a pause, but then she nodded again.

Thomas didn't like the pause, but he figured it was the best he'd get, and he didn't have the time to argue. A missing sheriff would be noticed a lot quicker than anyone else, so if his plan was going to work, he needed to move fast.

He looked down at the cord wrapped around her hands, then he held up the handcuffs for her to see.

"If you try anything, I will shoot you."

She nodded, and Thomas unwrapped the cord from her wrists.

When he had the handcuffs secured, he stood, pulling her to her feet, and led her by the arm toward the door. Once outside, he walked her around to the driver's side of the cruiser, opened the rear door, and started to push her in.

When she saw Parks, she resisted, complaining behind the duct tape.

"No choice," Thomas said. "Now get in."

Maggie hesitated, but she got in.

Chapter Thirty-Four

Magnolia

Thomas slammed the door.

I looked over at Sheriff Parks. He had fallen forward, and his head, wrapped in blood-soaked paper towels, was pressed against the passenger seat in front of him, his neck bent back at an unnatural angle.

Thomas got in behind the wheel.

I reached up with my cuffed hands and tore the duct tape away from my mouth. "Thomas, there are other options."

Thomas stared at his lap for a moment before shaking his head and saying, "Please be quiet. I need to think."

His voice was calm, almost casual, but I felt its coldness in my chest.

I stayed quiet, wanting to keep him calm, and waited.

A few seconds passed. Thomas took a deep breath, sighing as he exhaled, then he started the engine and pulled out of the parking lot.

I turned toward Sheriff Parks, then reached out and touched his neck.

My hands were cuffed together, so I had to lean into him to do it, but I wanted to know if he was still alive. I hoped I'd find a pulse, but the paper towels were so thick that I couldn't be sure. I was about to check his wrist when Thomas spoke.

"Don't bother, he's dead."

Again, the flat tone of his voice chilled me, and I sat back.

"Why are you doing this?"

"Why am I doing this?" He looked back at me in the rearview mirror. "The real question is why are you doing this."

"What are you talking about?"

"Why did you send him to ask me questions? I thought you trusted me."

I opened my mouth to explain, but then I thought better of it.

"I did everything right," he said. "I helped you find that ugly box, and you even kissed me after."

"Kissed you?"

He ignored me. "We were becoming friends, maybe more than friends someday, but then you told Parks that you didn't trust me."

"Thomas, I—"

"Why did you have to send him?"

"Send him?"

"Why did you do it?"

I hesitated, said, “Because you lied to me.”

This seemed to stop him. His grip tightened on the steering wheel, and I heard the leather moan beneath his fingers.

I waited for him to say something else. When he didn’t, I turned toward the window and focused on the road outside, forcing myself to breathe, to stay calm.

I watched the buildings pass by outside, hoping for a clue to where he was taking me, but I knew it was pointless. I’d only been in town a few days, and other than a handful of places along the boardwalk, I didn’t know any of the landmarks. We could be going anywhere, and I wouldn’t know where until we arrived.

It wasn’t until we turned onto a dirt road and started to climb that I had an idea where we might be heading.

“We’re going to the cliffs?”

Thomas glanced at me in the mirror. He stared for a moment, then turned back to the road and said, “Your sister trusted me.”

“She trusted everyone.” I paused, added, “I’m not her.”

“No.” He laughed under his breath. “You’re not.”

“And I apologize for that, but Thomas, whatever you’re planning on doing, you don’t have to. We can fix all of this.”

“You’re also a liar.”

“We can go to the police, turn ourselves in and tell them—”

“Shut up.”

“Tell them we panicked, and that everything went out of control, but that—”

“Shut up! Shut up! Shut up! Shut up!”

His voice echoed inside the car, making me wince.

I sat back and waited, and by the time he stopped, I thought I knew what I had to do. Pushing him would be dangerous, but it would also make him careless.

I waited until he seemed to calm down, then leaned forward, as close to his ear as I could get, and I whispered, "I know about your note."

Thomas shook his head, his knuckles turning white on the steering wheel.

"I know what you wrote."

"No," he said. "Lilly, stop."

"Lilly?" I tried to keep my voice light, edged with laughter. "Lilly is gone, Thomas. Don't you remember? You wrote a note filled with lies and you pinned it to a pair of her underwear and left it for Mike to find. And he did find it, didn't he?"

"Stop."

"Do you remember what he did next?" I asked. "After you set things in motion, he attacked her, and even though she swore to him that the things you wrote weren't true, he still—" My voice cracked, and I bit down hard, trying to swallow the knot of razor blades in my throat. "He—he beat her to death, didn't he? He beat her and he choked her and he killed her, all because of you and your note. He killed her over a lie, and you—"

"No!"

"Tell me why you did it," I said. "Was it to get back at him for beating you up, for embarrassing you in front of Lilly? Was that why? Because you were ashamed?"

Thomas slammed on the brakes, and the car skidded to a stop on the dirt road. He grabbed the gun sitting in the passenger seat and turned around, pointing it at me. For an instant, I was convinced he would pull the trigger, and I closed my eyes, waiting.

"Look at me."

Slowly, I did.

Thomas's voice was sharp.

"I wasn't embarrassed," he said. "And I wasn't ashamed, not for me." His eyes narrowed. "I was ashamed for them, and they were the ones who should've been embarrassed, but they weren't. People like that never are." He stopped talking, shook his head, and then turned back around. "Forget it, none of that matters anymore. All of this is almost over."

I didn't like the sound of that, but I waited until we were moving again before saying, "I promise it's not too late."

"Oh, Maggie." Thomas laughed. "I think we both know how this ends."

Chapter Thirty-Five

When we reached the top of the cliffs, Thomas drove along the edge until we saw the overlook. There were spots to park, and a thin chain running low between small wooden poles designed to keep people and cars away from the edge.

Thomas drove up to the chain and stopped.

He shut off the engine and stared out at the darkness, not moving.

In the near silence I could hear the low rumble of the ocean and the hiss of the wind rushing over the cliffs.

Thomas didn't move.

After a minute or two, I sat up in the seat and said, "Thomas, let me out."

He looked back at me in the mirror, as if remembering I was there. Then he nodded and got out. When he opened my door, he reached in and grabbed the back of my shirt, pulling me out of the seat and throwing me down. I would've stayed on my feet, but I hit the chain and tripped, falling hard and striking my head against a rock on the ground.

A universe of tiny black stars exploded behind my eyes.

I tried to sit up, but the world spun around me.

Eventually, I got myself up to sitting. I felt a line of blood run down my cheek, and the ringing in my ears sounded like a scream. All I could do was close my eyes tight and wait for my vision to clear. Once it did, I looked around for Thomas.

At first I didn't see him, but then I noticed movement in the back of the cruiser. A moment later, Thomas came around the side, dragging Sheriff Parks.

I watched him pull Parks to the driver's door, then drop him, letting the body hit the ground. Thomas stood up straight, put a hand on his lower back, and stretched into it.

He glanced down at Sheriff Parks and then at me. "You got part of it right, you know."

My head was still swimming, and Thomas's voice was muffled by the wind and the sea and the ringing in my ears. I started to ask him what he meant, but he'd already moved on. I watched him grab Parks by the shoulders and lift him into the driver's seat.

It took a few tries, but eventually he got Parks behind the wheel.

Thomas leaned heavily against the car, and I could see his shoulders rising and falling with his breath. Soon, his breathing slowed, and he reached into the car, took the keys from the ignition, and walked around back to the trunk.

"My father used to beat my mother," he said. "Did you know that?"

"No."

"He did." Thomas opened the trunk, then turned to face me. "Most of the time, he'd do it in their bedroom where I wouldn't see, but not always. Sometimes he'd do it in front of me."

I kept quiet.

"He hit her with an iron once, right here." He brushed his finger across the bottom of his jaw. "Not sure why he did it. Maybe there wasn't a reason. It was hard to tell a lot of the time. It was just who he was."

I didn't know what to say, so I didn't say anything.

"She was so beautiful, and so smart, and he beat her like she was nothing." He exhaled, letting his shoulders drop. "But do you know the worst part? The worst part for me, at least?"

I shook my head.

"Knowing that she let him do it." Thomas frowned. "That was unforgivable."

"You can't blame her."

"I blame them both." His voice was loud. "After the first time she knew exactly what he was, and she still made the choice to stay. Maybe she thought it was what she deserved, but it—" His voice cracked, and he turned back to the trunk. "But it wasn't."

Thomas reached into the trunk and took out a red gas can.

When I saw it, a wave of panic rose up inside me.

"Thomas, what are you—"

"Lilly was the same way," he said. "She thought it was what she deserved, too."

I was focused on the gas can and barely heard him.

"I tried to show her that she didn't have to stay with him, just like I tried telling my mother before I started that fire, but it didn't do any good. When you believe you deserve the pain and the humiliation, you're already lost."

"What fire?"

Thomas waved the question away. "Old news," he said. "They sent me away over it, asked me questions every day, made me take ridiculous tests to try and figure out why I did what I did, but it was all pointless. I knew why I did what I did, and I told them. They just didn't listen."

"I'm listening now," I said. "Tell me."

"You don't care."

"No," I said. "But I'm curious."

Thomas stared at me, a slow smile forming at the corners of his lips. "That's the first honest thing you've said."

"Tell me why you did it."

"Because nothing was ever going to change," he said. "She wasn't going to leave him, and he was never going to stop. Eventually he was going to kill her, just like Mike would've eventually killed your sister. That's why I had to put a stop to it."

I wasn't sure I heard him right, and I let his words sink in while I watched him walk back to the driver's side, opening the gas can as he went.

Finally, I said, "What do you mean Mike would've eventually killed Lilly?"

Thomas ignored me.

He lifted the can and poured the gasoline over the top of the car. It came out fast, and the wind caught it, blowing it back, soaking him. He stepped away quickly, spitting and coughing. Then he set the can on the ground and bent forward, hands on knees, retching.

I waited until he stopped, then said, "Thomas, tell me what you meant."

Thomas shook his hands dry in the air, then he wiped them on the front of his shirt. "What I meant about what?"

"You said eventually Mike would've killed Lilly."

"Because it's true," he said. "You know it as well as I do."

Thomas picked up the gas can and turned back to the car. This time he poured the gasoline inside the car, out of the wind. He poured it over the seats, the dash, the floor, and Sheriff Parks. When the can was empty, he took it around to the open trunk, tossed it inside, and grabbed a road flare.

"It was you," I said. "You killed her."

He looked over at me, and I saw the answer in his eyes.

"She was already dead," he said. "Maybe not that night, but it wouldn't have been long. I just finished the job Mike started." He pointed at me with the flare. "You might like to know that she apologized to me before she died. She told me I'd been right all along. She finally understood."

I reached out for one of the wooden poles and used it to brace myself as I got to my feet. My head ached, but I barely noticed it beneath the rage.

Slowly, I stepped over the chain, moving toward him.

Thomas had his back to me, and he was looking down at the flare in his hand. I was less than ten feet from him when he turned around.

He took the gun from his belt and pointed it at me.

"I told you, if you tried anything, I would shoot you." He cocked his head to the side, birdlike. "You don't believe me?"

I stopped moving, but I didn't take my eyes off him.

"You killed Lilly."

"Step back," he said. "It's not your turn."

"It wasn't Mike," I said. "It was you."

Thomas reached up and pulled the slide back, loading a round in the chamber. "Last warning."

I stood there, feeling a line of blood run down my neck and trail away under my shirt. I let the pieces of what must've happened that night click into place, and then, slowly, I stepped back.

"All the way to the chain," he said. "And if you move again . . ."

I backed up until I felt the chain against my legs.

Thomas seemed satisfied. He lowered the gun and slid it under his belt. Then he turned his attention back to the road flare, striking it, trying to figure out how it worked.

"Do you feel any guilt at all?" I asked.

"Guilt?" He looked up at me. "All your sister had to look forward to was years of pain and abuse. I loved her, and I killed her out of love. I saved her."

"She was my sister," I said. "My best friend."

"She was broken!" Thomas's voice was sharp, and he stared at me, his shoulders rising and falling with his breath. "They both were, but that doesn't matter anymore. Don't you see? None of this matters."

He looked down at the flare and struck the end.

This time the flare blazed to life in a bright red flash.

Thomas jumped back, startled, and held the burning flare out in front of him. I saw him smile, briefly, proud of his accomplishment, but then the flames caught the spilled gasoline on his skin and quickly climbed up his arms to his chest.

Thomas panicked.

He dropped the flare and slapped at the front of his shirt, spreading the flames.

Then he began to scream.

I charged him, hitting him in the center of the chest with all my weight and pushing him backward. Thomas stumbled and fell into the open door of the cruiser. There was a loud sucking sound, and the car erupted in flame.

The force of the heat knocked me back, and I landed hard.

When I opened my eyes, my hands were on fire.

The pain screamed up my arms, and I rolled on the ground, smothering the flames underneath me. When I was sure the fire was out, I sat up and looked down at my hands.

The skin was red and blistering.

That's when Thomas started shooting.

He was standing beside the cruiser, weaving back and forth, the top half of his body engulfed in flames. He fired aimlessly. I heard one of the bullets whistle past my head. Another struck the wooden post beside me. The rest went wild.

Then the gun clicked empty.

I pushed myself up and ran toward the cruiser.

The flames inside the cab burned the air, and I went around to the trunk. I found the fire extinguisher right where I knew it would be. I didn't know if it would put the flames out, but I had to try.

As I came around the car, Thomas stopped screaming.

I looked over and saw the gun fall from his hand. It landed on the ground beside his feet, and then he dropped to his knees as the flames danced over his blackening skin.

I pulled the pin on the extinguisher and began spraying the inside of the cruiser.

And Thomas?

I let him burn.

Chapter Thirty-Six

The fire department was the first to arrive, followed by an ambulance and two sheriff's deputies. I sat on the back bumper of the ambulance, watching the firefighters put out what was left of the blaze, while one of the paramedics wrapped my hands in wet bandages. When she finished, I thanked her and tried to get up.

She put a hand on my shoulder, stopping me. "You need to have a doctor look at those burns."

"I'm fine," I said. "They don't hurt."

"That's good," the paramedic said. "But they will."

She was right.

By the time we arrived at the hospital, the adrenaline had worn off, and my hands felt like the skin was slowly being peeled away from my flesh. The pain was unrelenting, and when the nurse injected something into my IV and told me it would help, I didn't know whether to laugh or cry.

Instead, I closed my eyes and waited.

Within seconds, the pain faded.

I was enjoying the ride on the painkillers, when I heard someone say my name.

I opened my eyes and saw a deputy standing beside my bed. He was young, not much older than me, and he had a wide-eyed, stunned look on his face that made me think he was traveling uncharted territory.

"Miss James, I need to ask you a few questions." He opened a notepad and took a pen from his breast pocket. "It'll only take a minute."

It took longer.

I answered his questions and went over everything that happened, starting with my arrival at the Orion Motor Lodge that night. I explained my theory about the note, my conversation with Sheriff Parks, and why I'd asked him to meet me there. But when I got to the drive up to the top of the cliffs, and Thomas's confession, I stopped talking.

The deputy waited.

I thought about seeing Lilly in this same hospital, in that cold room several floors below. I thought about my sister, my best friend, and what Mike had done to her, what Thomas had done to her. Then I thought of the child she once was, and a bright summer day beside the pool, standing next to her, feeling her hand in mine.

Don't be scared, Magnolia.

"Miss James?" The deputy was watching me. "What did he say to you?"

I looked up at him, and I could feel the words in my throat, waiting to come out.

But I didn't let them.

Thomas was dead, and Lilly was dead, and even though Mike didn't kill her, he was as responsible for what happened to her as the rest of us.

The realization made my decision easier.

I would let the dead bury the dead.

"Nothing," I said. "He didn't say anything."

The deputy's eyes narrowed, and I could tell he didn't believe me. He was about to say something else when I heard a familiar voice from outside in the hall.

Clay Jenkins stepped into the room.

He looked from me to the deputy, then said, "You done?"

"Yes, sir," the deputy said. "Just about."

Clay came closer, never taking his eyes off me. He must've seen something in my face, because he frowned, then turned to the deputy and said, "You're done."

This time it wasn't a question.

The deputy hesitated, and for a second it looked like he might argue, but he didn't. Instead, he held a small manila envelope out to me.

"We found this at the scene," he said. "We think it belonged to your sister."

I started to reach for it, but my hands were cocooned in bandages, so Clay took the envelope and said, "Give us a minute, will you?"

Again, the deputy looked like he wanted to argue, but instead he turned to me and said, "If you'd like to change your statement, Miss James, you can call the station."

I thanked him, then watched him walk out.

Once he was gone, I couldn't help but smile.

"What could possibly be funny?" Clay asked.

"You and that deputy," I said. "Once the boss, always the boss."

Clay made a low grumbling noise, then he held up the envelope.

I nodded, and watched as he opened the flap at the top. He looked inside, glanced at me briefly, then he reached in and pulled out a long chain and a silver key.

Both were scorched black.

He held the chain out, the key dangling in the air between us.

I stared at it for a long time.

Then I began to cry.

The next morning the doctors replaced the bandages with gauze, making it easier to use my hands, and I left the hospital soon after.

Clay gave me a ride to my hotel.

"What are you going to do now?" he asked. "Any plans?"

"I'm not sure," I said. "I don't want to go back to Lilly's apartment, so I'll most likely go home."

Clay adjusted himself in his seat, and I could tell he wanted to say something, but he didn't, and we drove the rest of the way in silence. When we pulled up in front of the Cliff House, he put the car in park, then turned to look at me.

"Before you leave, I'd appreciate it if you went to see Ava," he said. "If I let you go without saying goodbye to her, I'd never hear the end of it."

I smiled. "I will."

Clay nodded. "Listen, I—" He stopped, inhaled deeply, looked away. "Manitou Springs, right? What will you do there?"

"Haven't decided."

"Family or friends back there?"

"No," I said. "Not really."

"No one?"

"Only ghosts."

Again, Clay looked like he wanted to say something, but the words wouldn't come. I waited, just in case, and then leaned over and wrapped my arms around his neck.

I squeezed him tight, whispered, "Thank you."

Clay patted me on the shoulder.

When we broke, he motioned to the front of the hotel and said, "You better go inside. I—" His voice cracked. He cleared his throat, tried again. "I've got things to do."

That afternoon I stood on the balcony and looked out over the sea. The day was bright and as clear as a bell, and the salty air felt cool and crisp against my skin.

I stayed out there for a long time.

When I finally went in, I took the manila envelope from the table, opened the flap, and turned it over, letting Lilly's charred key slide out into my hand.

I turned it over a few times, rubbing away what was left of the black, then I crossed the room to my backpack sitting in the corner. I unzipped the top and pulled out my mother's ivory jewelry box. Then I unzipped a smaller compartment on the side of the backpack, reached in, and took out another silver key on another silver chain.

Almost identical, but not quite.

I sat on the edge of the bed, the two keys in my hands, studying them. I put them together, side by side, and pressed until I heard the familiar click, then I picked up the box and slid this new key into the lock.

It opened.

Slowly, I lifted the lid.

The first thing I saw was a postcard, worn and faded. The photo on the front showed the Golden Gate Bridge with Alcatraz and the San Francisco skyline half hidden in a low white fog. I turned it over, saw it was addressed to my mother, and recognized my father's handwriting.

It's cold here without you.
All my love,
Alex

There were other postcards—New York, Austin, Chicago, along with a stack of handwritten letters, all from my father to my mother. The postmarks on the envelopes were from before Lilly and I were born.

I set the letters on the bed beside me and turned back to the box.

My mother's engagement ring was inside along with the antique emerald broach, and a black pearl necklace. I picked up the necklace, ran the pearls between my fingers like a rosary, and for a brief moment I remembered her face. Then the image faded, slipping away like smoke.

Everything my mother had left behind was in that box.

Lilly hadn't pawned any of it.

Chapter Thirty-Seven

On my last night in Beaumont Cove, I left the hotel and walked along the boardwalk. The sky was clear and full of stars, and a heavy moon hung low over the horizon, reflecting a silver path across the surface of the sea. I stopped a couple of times to stand at the railing, lean into the ocean breeze, and let the sight fill me.

There was one more person I needed to say goodbye to, but I wasn't in a hurry to see her. Part of me realized that once I said goodbye, I'd have nothing left to do in Beaumont Cove, and it would be time to go home.

So I took my time.

When I reached her building, the store was quiet and the windows were dark.

I felt a sharp stab of regret in the pit of my stomach, and I cursed myself for not coming by sooner. My bus wasn't scheduled to leave until ten the next morning, so I thought there was a chance I could catch her before I left. If not, I would have to call once I made it home.

Clay had given me their number, and I'd already promised to stay in touch.

I hated the idea of leaving without seeing Ava again, but I knew all too well that life didn't always give you the chance to say goodbye.

Before I turned away, I decided to try the door. I didn't think it would be unlocked, but I'd walked all that way, and I didn't want to go back without checking.

As I got closer to the door, the silver-white eye in the window lit up, and the neon **OPEN** sign flickered to life.

I smiled, not at all surprised.

When I stepped through the split curtain into the main room, Ava was alone on the couch. She had a book open on her lap, and there were three white candles burning on the end table beside her. When she saw me, she took off her cat-eye glasses, smiled, and closed her book.

"Sometime you'll have to explain your Open-sign trick to me."

"What do you mean?"

I started to explain, then changed my mind. "Never mind."

"Did you come for your reading?"

"I came to say goodbye."

"You're leaving?"

"Tomorrow morning."

Ava didn't say anything, and she didn't look away.

I tried to pretend that it didn't make me feel uncomfortable, her watching me like that, but it did. As much as I hated to admit it, I wasn't looking forward to going back to Manitou, and I think she knew it. There were too many memories for me there, too many empty spaces that had once been filled by people I loved.

Going back felt like returning to a life that no longer existed.

"We'll be sad to see you go," Ava said. "Are you sure it's what you want?"

I tried to smile and failed. "I'm not sure about anything."

Ava nodded, set her book on the end table beside her, and said, "I think I know a way to clear things up."

I was about to tell her that as much as I liked her, the last thing I wanted was a reading, but before the words were out of my mouth, Ava reached into her pocket and took out a joint.

This time I didn't have to try to smile.

"Come on," she said. "Grab a seat."

I walked over and sat in one of the chairs beside the couch. "I thought you were going to offer me a reading."

"Would you like one?"

There was hope in her voice, but I shook my head.

"I didn't think so." She lifted one of the candles, lit the joint, inhaled, and handed it to me. "You seem to be in a place that requires deeper thought."

I took my turn, and for a while we passed the steadily shrinking joint back and forth, talking, telling warm stories about Lilly, and laughing.

"Can I ask you something?"

"Of course," Ava said, holding in the smoke.

"Why do people around here call you the witch?"

She exhaled, coughed. "You've heard that?"

"Even Clay calls you that."

Ava laughed. "I like to think it's a term of endearment."

"Is that all?" I asked. "No real reason?"

"Well, I can't say for sure." She handed me the joint. "You live your life and you do what you can to add a little spice and mystery to a town, and for a while everyone is happy and everything seems fine." She paused, held up one finger. "But you drink the blood of one infant . . ."

I nearly choked.

We laughed for a long time.

When I could breathe again, I sat back in the chair and said, "I'm glad I got to see you before I left."

"Me too," she said. "Now, I have a question for you."

I nodded, waited.

"Have you considered staying?"

"Ah," I said. "I don't think—"

"I get it," she said. "You haven't exactly seen the town at its best, but it's a fine place at its core, and it's weird enough to never get boring."

I handed her the joint. "I can see that."

"The Cove has its own special charm," she said. "Some people say it's haunted."

"Haunted?"

She nodded. "In time, you'll make up your own mind on that one. For now, let me just say that I think you'll fit in perfectly around here."

The idea of staying felt warm in my chest, but I still wasn't sure, and I told her so.

"Did Clayton tell you he's running for sheriff?"

"Is he really?"

"They're holding an emergency election to replace Parks," she said. "I think he's too old, but when one of his wacky ideas takes hold of him, he doesn't listen to me."

"I think it's a great idea."

Ava made a dismissive sound. "Of course you do. Thick as thieves already." She looked down at what was left of the joint, then took another from her pocket and lit it off the first. "If he does become sheriff again, I'll need a new partner." She looked at me. "How about it? Interested?"

"Partner?"

"To take Clayton's place."

"I don't understand."

"Sure you do." She put the joint to her lips, inhaled, then handed it to me. "Sometimes people with questions need a psychic. Other times, they need a private investigator."

I laughed. "I knew you and Clay had some kind of arrangement."

"It's not as shady as all that," she said. "Truth is, sometimes I don't have the answers people are looking to find, and it's the same with him. Where one of us falls short, the other can usually fill in the blanks."

"So when someone comes to you because they think their spouse is cheating?"

"If the cards don't show the answer, the camera usually will," she said. "You know how these things work. You've done the job before."

She was right, I had done the job before, but in a place I'd lived my entire life, and with my father standing over my shoulder. Starting out on my own, in a completely new town, was something else entirely.

"I wouldn't even know where to begin."

"We already have the office space," Ava said. "And Clayton will be around to lend a hand until you get your feet under you. He's already told me he plans on helping you get your license."

"He said that?"

"It was his idea."

I thought about it, and I was surprised to find I was actually considering it.

And why not?

There was no one waiting for me in Manitou Springs, nothing to keep me there. Why go back when everywhere I looked, all I'd see were shadows of the past?

I thought about the first time I saw Beaumont Cove. It'd been through a rain-streaked bus window as we crested the hills to the south. I remembered how the town seemed to unfurl along the beach beneath those bone-white cliffs, appearing as if it had been hidden from sight, and had chosen that moment to reveal itself.

Welcome to the edge of the world.

Beyond this place there be dragons.

There was something comforting about the memory, and for the first time I thought I understood what Lilly had seen in this place, and why she'd decided to stay.

Beaumont Cove belonged to her.

It belonged to her the way it belonged to all of the lost and the left behind. The way it now belonged to me.

A forgotten town for forgotten people.

"Well?" Ava was waiting for my answer. "What do you say?"

"I say it's a big decision."

She smiled, showing her gold tooth. "Then you're at the right place. I specialize in big decisions."

I laughed. "You think the universe has an answer for me?"

"I wouldn't presume to say," she said. "But I've never seen the harm in asking."

I stayed quiet, and Ava watched me, waiting to see which way I'd fall.

In the end, I gave in.

"Okay," I said. "One reading."

Ava nearly squealed. She clapped her hands in front of her face and stood up.

"But don't think this is going to become a regular thing," I said, getting to my feet. "I still don't believe any of this stuff."

"I understand."

"I'm serious, Ava."

"I know you are," she said. "And we'll work on that."

I opened my mouth, but before I could say anything else, she stepped in and looped her arm through mine, gently leading me away.

"Come on, Magnolia," she said. "Let's see what we can see."

ACKNOWLEDGMENTS

Thank you to Gracie Doyle, Jessica Tribble Wells, Caitlin Alexander, Laura Barrett, Christopher Lin, and the entire Thomas & Mercer team. Thank you to my early readers, Peter Farris, Kimberly Collison, and Paul Garth. Thank you to my family for putting up with a husband and father who spends far too much time in his imagination. And thank you to my nieces, Ava Joy and Magnolia James, for the use of their names. Finally, I'd like to thank all the readers who've stuck with me over the last ten years. It's been a blast.

ABOUT THE AUTHOR

John Rector is the bestselling author of *The Grove*, *The Cold Kiss*, *Already Gone*, *Out of the Black*, *Ruthless*, and *The Ridge*. Rector's short fiction has appeared in numerous magazines and has won several awards, including the International Thriller Award for the novella *Lost Things*. For more information, visit www.johnrector.blogspot.com.